CONVOY NORTH

Other novels in the *Convoy* series

CONVOY NORTH

Philip McCutchan

St. Martin's Griffin
New York

Library of Congress Cataloging-in-Publication Data

McCutchan, Philip
    Convoy north / Philip McCutchan.
        p.   cm.
    ISBN 0-312-14298-6
    1. World War, 1939–1945—Naval operations, British—
Fiction.   2. Great Britain—History, Naval—20th
century—Fiction.   I. Title.
[PR6063.A167C65   1996]
823'.914—dc20   96-2253
                                                     CIP

First published in Great Britain by
George Weidenfeld & Nicolson Limited

First St. Martin's Griffin Edition: May 1996

10   9   8   7   6   5   4   3   2   1

CONVOY NORTH

ONE

The cold was bitter; men's breath crackled from their lips. As yet, no ice had formed on the fo'c'sles of the ships in convoy or on the decks and lifeboats; but that would come soon enough, even before they raised the North Cape at the tip of Norway and headed into the Barents Sea and the terrible conditions of the Arctic winter. Commodore John Mason Kemp paced the bridge of the ss *Hardraw Falls*, a heavy duffel coat covering the bridge coat with the thick gold stripe and the interlaced 'curl' of the Royal Naval Reserve on the shoulders, thinking ahead, planning in advance what his moves should be in any imaginable situation, prepared so that every vital second should be saved when trouble came. As Commodore of the convoy he was responsible for the conduct of the merchant ships, eighteen of them all told, shepherded along the route to Russia by an escort of two cruisers and four destroyers plus a group of anti-submarine trawlers and corvettes. Not a very strong escort; but the best that could be mustered by an overstretched British fleet against the might of the German Navy that would stand between them and the port of Archangel – or Murmansk if the big winter freeze, predicted by the Met men to be coming later this winter than was usual, should in the event confound the forecasts – and between Kemp's duty to deliver vital war supplies to the embattled Russian armies that were trying to block the eastward thrust of Hitler's Panzer divisions.

In the fading light, Kemp looked astern. Moving out from Hvalfiord in the early morning, they had steamed north about past Ondverdharnes and Bjargtangar to take their final departure from Norway from Straumnes. Now they were standing

1

clear for the northern ocean wastes behind the A/S group, with the heavy cruisers *Nottingham* and *Neath* out on either beam, the destroyers moving astern to form the rearguard.

'Commodore, sir?'

Kemp turned. 'Yes, Cutler?'

'All clear ahead, sir.'

'In what respect?'

'Situation report from the Admiralty,' Cutler said.

'Say so, then. An incomplete report's worse than none at all, Cutler. All clear ahead – that could mean anything.'

'Sorry, sir.'

Kemp nodded and grinned. 'All right, Cutler.' The Commodore's assistant tore off a salute, a curious one that Kemp had not yet acclimatized himself to: it was a movement of a vertically-held hand across the face, the fingers almost touching the nose, a parody of an American style salute. Thomas B. Cutler was in fact an American, from Texas of all places, cow country, not a wave in sight. But Cutler had been dead keen to join the war in which his country was not yet involved, and he'd seen that the best way of doing so was to join the Royal Canadian Naval Volunteer Reserve. A thrustful young man, he had achieved this against many difficulties. Kemp admired his courage in joining in the war when he had no need to. Kemp believed he had got himself a very useful assistant, but Cutler had a thing or two to learn yet. However, it was good news that the Admiralty had nothing on the plot.

So far.

Kemp glanced across at the *Hardraw Falls'* master. Captain Ezekiel Theakston was a Yorkshireman and looked it. A strong, square face, not truculent but determined and forming the window of a mind very much its own. Theakston had already told Kemp, back at the convoy conference some while before, that he came from Whitby, the birthplace of Captain Cook, who had been his boyhood hero. Kemp believed that Captain Theakston had told him this because the Commodore had been a peacetime master in the Mediterranean-Australia Line, which he wouldn't have been, presumably, if Cook had never discovered Australia. .... Theakston had spoken of his hero in such a way that he had managed to sound as though he himself in some former existence had been jointly responsible for the voyage of

2

exploration. Perhaps, Kemp thought, this was a manifestation of being a Yorkshireman.

ii

The PQ convoy had assembled off the island of Mull at the northern end of the Firth of Lorne ten days earlier, and the convoy conference had been held in the port of Oban. Captain Theakston had come to this conference by train from Whitby, the *Hardraw Falls* having been sailed north from Liverpool by his chief officer, Ben Amory. Captain Theakston had obtained compassionate leave because his wife, Dora, had been seriously ill; he believed she had now turned the corner but in any case he had had to leave her to rejoin his ship before the convoy finally sailed from the United Kingdom. War was all-consuming and didn't wait for mariners' wives to recover. Dora Theakston didn't carry much weight in the scales against the munitions requirements of Marshal Stalin, and Captain Theakston was a man who took his duty seriously. He looked down at his wife as she lay in bed, as he might into an open hold to ensure that his chief officer had been attentive to the stowing of the cargo; and he saw that indeed she carried very little weight and never mind Marshal Stalin. She was all skin and bone, but he didn't mention this to her.

'You'll do, lass,' he said.

'Yes, Ezekiel. You're not to worry.'

'You know I will.' Dora was fifty-three and currently looked twenty years older. 'I'll be back the moment we dock. Amory's a good man, and can be left in charge again.' He bent and kissed her and left immediately. A backward glance from the door, a brief pause, showed him a grieving woman and a lonely one who would worry about him without cease, all the time he was gone. No children – a pity, now. Not that they hadn't tried, but Dora wasn't a childbearing woman it seemed, even though she came of a big family herself, one of eleven offspring of a dales farmer – oddly enough from Cotterdale near Hardraw Falls. A coincidence, that, and Theakston thought it could even have some significance; he wished he could read the mind of God.

Grim-faced, Captain Theakston embarked on the long journey

3

north, taking the train from Whitby to York where he caught the express for Edinburgh and then travelled on to Perth and thence via Kinross to Oban, and the convoy conference where he and the other assembled masters were addressed by an officer of the Naval Control Service staff, a lieutenant-commander RNR who had given them their route and detailed convoy orders. Theakston had listened attentively, as he had done when Commodore Kemp had taken over and introduced himself, an informal talk and a welcome to the man he was to sail with. Captain Theakston, who knew already that his ship was to wear the broad pennant of the convoy Commodore, had been pleased to learn at the same time that the Commodore was genuine RNR: Theakston had no love for the RN, and with foul luck might have drawn a retired admiral serving in the rank of Commodore RNR for the duration. There were plenty such officers with much experience of bull but none of the ways of the merchant ships and the men who sailed them in peace and war.

After the conference, Theakston found himself alongside Kemp, a man built like a bear, a big bear with a kindly face. Theakston said, 'I reckon we'll get on.'

'I hope so, Captain.'

'Aye. I'm told you're a liner man, Mediterranean-Australia.'

'Yes.' That was when Kemp heard about Whitby; and learned that Captain Theakston, whose uniform jacket, like that of Kemp himself, bore a row of medal ribbons from the previous war, had been with Bricker Dockett Steamships of Hull from third officer to master, a matter of twenty-nine years now.

'A long time,' Kemp said pleasantly.

'Aye, it's been that.' Captain Theakston gave him a look that said he'd made a trite remark and might have saved his breath. Kemp grinned to himself: he'd always heard that Yorkshiremen were blunt in speech. Now he knew this one was blunt in facial expression as well.

iii

Sub-Lieutenant Thomas B. Cutler, RCNVR – 'Tex' to a wide variety of friends – had spent the night before the conference ashore in Oban's Station Hotel. He had spent it with a girl he'd met the previous day in the Central Hotel in Glasgow. He'd bumped into her, literally, soon after he'd got off the train from Euston. Right in the hotel entrance he'd almost knocked her over with his grip. He'd swept off his cap with a flourish and apologized handsomely.

'My fault, ma'am. I'm an oaf.'

'An American oaf by the sound. What's that uniform?'

He sang it to her. 'If you ask us who we are, We're the RCNVR ...' The tune was 'Roll Along, Covered Wagon'. 'But don't let it worry you. Just call me Tex.'

The girl giggled, a friendly sound. They looked at each other. She appeared to be at a loose end. Cutler spotted the bar.

'How's about a drink?' he asked.

She nodded, and he put a hand on her elbow and guided her into the bar. They sat at a table for two, in a corner. He saw she was wearing a wedding ring and noted also that she already had a drink or two inside her.

He asked, 'What's it to be?'

'Scotch, please.'

At the bar he ordered two doubles and carried them back to the table. He knew he was lucky to get whisky so easily in wartime Britain, but this after all was Scotland and probably the Scots saw to it that not too much of their life-blood crossed the border when it was scarce.

He said interrogatively, 'Well?'

'Well, what?'

'I've told you I'm Tex. You?'

She shrugged. 'Roz,' she said, sounding indifferent.

'Two nice single syllables. Roz anything else?' Cutler lifted an eyebrow. She didn't answer; he laid a finger on her left hand, on the wedding ring. 'Ma'am,' he said earnestly, very American now, 'I don't reckon to drink with women whose husbands might show at any moment. Not drink too long, that is. Some husbands might not like it.'

'It's all right,' she said. Her fingers shook a little, the voice became clipped. She drank the double Scotch quickly and then confided. Her husband had been in the RAF, a squadron leader, and two months earlier he'd been shot down in his Spitfire over the eastern counties. Roz had drifted since then. No children, not married long, no parents living ... currently she was stay-

5

ing in Glasgow with an aunt who was something in the wvs and was often away, as she was now. They had more drinks and Roz became tearful. They had dinner but she had no appetite. That night she went up with him to his room and next day, since she had nowhere else to go other than her aunt's flat, the empty flat, she went with him on the train to Oban and they booked into the Station Hotel.

iv

Aboard the *Hardraw Falls* lying at anchor in the Firth of Lorne Chief Officer Amory looked across the water at the hard outline of Mull to port, at the Argyll hills to starboard, hills that ran down easterly towards Loch Awe and a slice of Scottish history – Campbell country, and Amory's mother had been a Campbell from Portsonachan. Amory had spent summer holidays there in his schooldays; he wished he was there now, looking across the summer blue of a loch that could grow grey and angry in winter, across towards the ancient stronghold of Kilchurn Castle. But wishing would get him nowhere. He smacked a horny palm against the teak rail of the bridge and went below to his cabin to go once again through his cargo manifests, wondering if the Old Man would ever wring a proper signature of receipt from the Russians. The manifest *in toto* ran to many pages and each entry concerned materials of war – ammunition, explosives, guns and gun parts. The *Hardraw Falls* was loaded to her marks, ten thousand tons of mostly HE, a fine place, Amory thought, to put the Convoy Commodore. One unlucky hit by the Nazis and it would be a case of finito. But then almost all the rest of the convoy would be carrying similar cargoes. You didn't take toys to Russia in wartime . . . some of the ships carried foodstuffs, grain and so on, but they weren't fitted out to take the Commodore and his staff. There was a tanker, but she would be equally at risk, and in any case she was a Royal Fleet Auxiliary and thus officially part of the naval escort, no direct concern of the Commodore.

After a while Amory gathered up his papers and shoved them away in a drawer. He lit a cigarette and drew in a lungful of smoke, pushing himself back at arm's length from his desk. His glance fell on three photographs in silver frames: his mother

6

and father, taken some years before – his father was wearing the uniform of a police superintendent. Amory grinned to himself: his father had always been a copper, on and off duty, never let up, do this, do that, get your hair cut, don't come home late, where have you been ... no doubt it had been good training and had helped the young Ben Amory through a tough sea apprenticeship lasting four years plus. But it hadn't made home life easy and it had worn his mother out, worn her literally to death.

The third photograph was of a young woman. She, too, was dead: a Nazi bomb on London, back in the days of the Battle of Britain, more than a year ago now. Ben Amory had considered himself a confirmed bachelor until he had met Felicity, who was some years younger than himself and had captivated him from his first sight of her. They hadn't married: Hitler had beaten the banns. So bachelordom was back. Amory knew there would never be anybody else. He had picked up the silver frame when a knock came at his door.

He put the frame down as though caught out in some guilty act. 'Yes?'

It was the watchman from the gangway. 'Boat coming off from Oban, sir.'

'Approaching us?'

'Yes, sir. Could be the Captain.'

'I'll be down.' Amory got to his feet and reached for his cap. He followed the watchman down to the starboard accommodation ladder, arriving at the upper platform just as the boat came alongside. A bulky figure stepped out first and climbed fast to the upper platform, followed by Captain Theakston. There was a naval cap badge and a row of brass oak leaves on the cap's peak: the Commodore. Amory saluted awkwardly. Theakston made the introductions, including in them a young officer wearing wavy stripes who had come up behind him.

'All ready, Mr Amory?'

'Yes, sir.'

'Good.' Captain Theakston looked briefly fore and aft along the embarkation deck. 'The convoy leaves at 0100 hours. Be ready to shorten-in at half an hour after midnight, Mr Amory.'

'Aye, aye, sir.'

The sky was darkening already, the early northern evening setting in. The last of the sun glinted from the snow-clad Scottish

7

hillsides, shafted across dull grey water between the arms of the land. The water was still, no wind at all, and there was a hint of fog about to come down to make the outward passage tricky. The ships lay ghostlike, the naval escort taking on a sinister look, lean and grey and with their guns neatly trained to the fore-and-aft line. They wouldn't stay that way for long. The Russian convoys had started quietly enough but the Nazis were known by now to have built up their destroyer and U-boat strength in the northern waters.

Theakston stumped up the ladders to his quarters below the bridge, accompanied by the Commodore and Sub-Lieutenant Cutler. Entering his cabin he pressed a bell for his steward.

'My compliments to Mr Paget and I'd like to see him at once. And Mr Buckle.'

'Yes, sir.' The steward left the master's cabin. Kemp looked around, feeling in need of a short drink. No offer was forthcoming, and no apology. Captain Theakston, Kemp reflected, had the look of a teetotaller. No bad thing, of course, and not to be faulted. But teetotallers tended to make prickly shipmates. Kemp caught Cutler's eye and refrained from winking back at the grin he saw on his assistant's face. Cutler evidently had the same thought. Until Paget and Buckle had reported, Theakston said little other than to indicate chairs for Kemp and Cutler. Paget, the second officer and thus responsible for navigation, was told to lay off a course through the Minch for Hvalfiord in Norway.

'We call in there, Mr Paget.'

'Yes, sir.'

'Go and get on with it, then.' Next came Buckle, the ship's chief steward. The accommodation for the Commodore and his staff was ready, he said. He would show Commodore Kemp to the master's spare cabin. Theakston grunted and waved a hand : Kemp gathered he was dismissed, and took his departure.

v

In addition to Cutler, Kemp's staff consisted of a leading signalman and an ordinary signalman, a telegraphist and a number of gunnery rates – a petty officer with the non-substantive rate of

8

seaman gunner in charge of a leading seaman and ten hands to man the ship's armament, which wasn't much: close-range AA weapons – Bofors, Lewis guns, Oerlikons, mounted in the bridge wings, on monkey's island above the wheelhouse and chart room, and aft above the engineers' accommodation. The other ships in convoy carried similar armament; the main defence would be the escort. Aboard the Commodore's ship, Petty Officer Napper was the man in charge of the weaponry and his sour, horse-like face said he didn't go much on it. No use complaining though; it was the best that could be allocated, no doubt of that. There were always shortages. In fact PO Napper was inclined to be sour about taking valuable war material to Russia when Britain herself stood in need of it.

'Bloody bolshies,' he said to Leading Signalman Corrigan in the compartment allocated as the naval messdeck. 'Hitler's allies, not long since. Probably change again before long.'

Corrigan didn't waste breath answering. Hitler's hordes advancing like Attila the Hun across the Russian land mass had put paid to any thoughts of another Nazi–Communist get-together, and now Russia had to be treated as a full member of the Allies against the Axis powers. Napper went on chuntering away to himself, a regular old woman Corrigan thought, though they'd met for the first time only in RNB Pompey when they'd been detailed by the drafting master-at-arms to form the party for the *Hardraw Falls*. Napper was an RFR man, a Fleet Reservist, and looked it, grey-faced and wrinkled, not far off fifty, too old to be still at sea. Napper's bunk was piled high with home comforts extracted from his kit-bag: mufflers, balaclavas, seaboot stockings – fair enough, of course. But the rest! There was a tea-cosy, currently filled with an assortment of medicines. Corrigan had seen Enos, Carter's Little Liver Pills, a packet of senna pods, aspirins, a tin of Germoline, corn plasters and a small corn knife, and a bottle of Dr J. Collis Browne's Chlorodyne, presumably in case the senna pods worked too well.

Napper saw Corrigan looking at it all.

'What's up?'

'Nothing, PO. Just hope you won't be needing it, that's all.'

'It's the wife,' Napper said defensively.

'Looks after you, does she?'

'That's her job, isn't it?' Napper began to push things

straight, looked round and found a drawer beneath the bunk. He opened it and began stowing away his medicine chest. He gave a sudden cough, and stopped to feel his chest. Buggeration – his weak point! And sod the war. He rooted about, found some camphorated oil. Better not rub it in now, the air up top was enough to freeze the balls off a brass monkey and he couldn't turn in yet, not until the convoy had weighed and the ships' companies had been fallen out to take up cruising stations. After midnight, that would be. Napper stood there uncertainly, with the camphorated oil in his hand, and coughed again. His face looked hollow with anxiety.

Corrigan grinned. He said, 'Big decision, eh, PO?'

'What d'you mean?'

'To rub or not to rub.'

Napper glared. 'What do *you* know about it?'

'More than you think, PO.'

Napper shoved the bottle out of sight. That Corrigan . . . there was a posh accent. The wartime navy had brought in all manner of different people, not a bit like peacetime. Corrigan, a hostilities-only rating, was a convoy signalman, something a shade different from a proper naval bunting tosser, a shorter qualifying course, and some of them were posh, so he'd been told, aiming for commissions as sub-lieutenants RNVR. 'You a college boy?' he asked.

'That depends on what you mean by college, PO.'

'I don't want any of your lip.'

'It wasn't meant to be lip, PO, just a statement of fact. It so happens I was a medical student . . . I wanted to get into the war so I chucked it, anyway till the war's over.'

Napper's lips framed a whistle. 'Makee-learn doctor, was you?'

'That's right.'

'Then you know all about camphorated oil.'

'A little,' Corrigan answered modestly. Petty Officer Napper rubbed reflectively at a blue-shaded jowl. This bunting tosser was a find and he'd never had such luck before. His own medical adviser, right on the spot! Worth keeping in with, worth buttering up in fact. Free advice. . . .

'What do you advise?' he asked anxiously. 'It's me chest, you see. Got a cough.' He lit a fag and coughed some more. 'I had pleurisy, once. Don't want to get it again. Then there's the bowels, see. Not reg'lar . . .'

vi

'Escort taking up station, sir.'

'Thank you, Corrigan.' Kemp turned to Captain Theakston, a thickset shadow in the dim light from the binnacle behind. 'All ready, Captain?'

'Aye, all ready. Mr Paget?'

'Yes, sir – '

'Pass to the fo'c'sle, shorten-in to three shackles.'

Paget passed the order down and the sound of the windlass, steam driven, came back to the men on the bridge, a rackety, clanking sound as the links of the cable came home up the hawse-pipe to drop down into the cable locker beneath the fo'c'sle accommodation. The senior officer of the escort, with his de-gaussing gear switched on, like all the other ships, against the possibility of magnetic mines, and paravanes ready to be streamed from either bow to deflect and cut the mooring cables that would attach any conventional mines to their sinkers, moved past to take up station ahead for moving out the convoy; when they were clear of the firth the cruisers would move out to the beam and leave the A/s group to sweep ahead of the merchant ships.

The windlass stopped and a shout came from Amory in the eyes of the ship: 'Shortened-in, sir, third shackle on deck.'

'Right.'

They waited. The darkness was thick but the fog was holding off, had not after all come down with the dark, thanks to a breeze that had come up to blow it away before it had properly formed. If that wind dropped, then the fog might come back. The water's surface was slightly ruffled and the breeze was a cold one – but the sea was cold too, otherwise the wind would have brought its own fog. Kemp sent up a prayer that it would hold off: no joke, navigating blind or by radar in pilotage waters, those of western Scotland in particular.

'Executive, sir.' This was Corrigan, watching the flagship's signal bridge.

11

'Thank you. Executive to all ships.'

'Aye, aye, sir.' Corrigan used his blue-shaded Aldis to flash the brief signal to the merchantmen in company, the signal that told the masters to proceed in execution of previous orders. Theakston gave the order to weigh anchor and once again the windlass started up, the wash-deck hoses in action to clean down the cable as it came slowly inboard under the eagle eye of Jock Tawney, the bosun, once again saying his farewells to Scotland ... he'd long since forgotten how many times he'd done that, though in the past it had been mainly the Clyde he'd sailed from.

Amory's voice came again from the fo'c'sle. 'Anchor's aweigh, sir.'

'Heave to the waterline, Mr Amory. Hold it on the brake.'

'Aye, aye, sir.' Until the ship was clear of the firth, the anchor would remain veered ready for letting go in an emergency: Theakston was a careful master.

Kemp said, 'We'll move to the head of the centre column, Captain.'

'I know that. I know the orders and this isn't my first convoy.'

'My apologies,' Kemp said. He cursed himself for a lack of tact. He would have to watch his step with Captain Theakston. The master, after all, commanded the ship, the Commodore of the convoy was a mere passenger until it fell to him to order the movements and manoeuvres of the convoy as a whole. As the *Hardraw Falls* began to move in response to the engine-room telegraph the other ships fell in astern on a sou'-sou'-westerly course to take them down towards Colonsay and the turn to starboard for the Dubh Artach light which they would leave away to port when they turned up for the Minch on passage north to Iceland.

The PQ convoy was away.

TWO

Always at the start of a convoy, of any sailing across the seas, there were the thoughts of home, many and varied. John Mason Kemp, by long experience of the sea life, was able to switch off the moment his ship was under way. The job needed concentration and so he concentrated. Before sailing he was as bad, as nostalgic as anyone else. He always hated leaving the cottage in Meopham, way down in Kent. He always had, even in peacetime, but it was that much worse with Hitler sending his *Luftwaffe* over to blast London and its environs – Meopham was scarcely an environ but was in the flight path from the airfields in occupied France and not all that far from targets such as RAF Biggin Hill. Then there were the simple facts of wartime life : the shortages ; the queues ; the making do ; the difficult lot of a wife left to cope on her own, not that Mary was unique in that respect, nor unique in having two sons as well as a husband involved in the war at sea. But she also had Kemp's aged grandmother to look after. No joke that, Kemp knew. Just before sailing from the Firth of Lorne, Kemp had reflected, as he had done many times before, that it was a curious situation for a middle-aged convoy commodore still to have someone to call granny. A pernickety one of well over ninety, not far off a hundred in fact, one of life's trials but a very game old bird.

Before going aboard the *Hardraw Falls* Kemp had rung his wife from the Station Hotel, a circumspect conversation with no places or ships mentioned since Hitler's ears were said to be everywhere, though a German agent in wartime Oban would have stood out like a bishop entering a brothel. Mary had seemed somewhat down and he'd chivvied her a little.

'It won't last for ever, Mary. Chin up!'

'It's not that,' she'd said.

'Ah! Granny?'

'Yes. She's been complaining – '

'She always does. What is it this time?'

'Oh . . . the cold, for one thing.' Kent could be cold and, like Scotland, often suffered snow problems, but not quite yet. 'She seems to feel it more and more.'

'Age,' Kemp said. He knew Mary had fuel problems: everyone was supposed to save gas and coal and electricity. 'Try not to worry . . . my shilling's run out,' he added as the pips went, 'and I haven't another. Sorry.'

'All right. Take care of yourself, John.'

'I'll do that,' he said, and the line went dead before he'd actually said goodbye. It was rather like an omen. He'd half a mind to ring back on a transferred charge call but it could take up to half an hour to be passed through all the exchanges that stood between Oban and Meopham and time was short. Leaving the telephone box, Kemp caught sight of his assistant, a new one whom he had met for the first time at the convoy conference. His assistant was doing two things: waiting for his lord and master and trying to disengage himself from a young woman with deep, dark rings under her eyes and an unsteady gait.

'All set, Cutler?' Kemp asked as he came up.

'All set, sir, Commodore.' He didn't look it by any means. Given any encouragement at all the girl would embark with him. 'Drifter's at the quay, sir.'

'Let's go, then.' Kemp felt he'd sounded like an American film: the rub-off already, just from knowing he had an American assistant? He fixed the young woman with his eye. 'Make short work of it,' he said, and headed for the hotel entrance that gave on to the quay, not far to go. He saw the drifter waiting and Captain Theakston, beneath a harbour lamp, holding an old-fashioned pocket-watch ostentatiously in front of his face. From behind he heard the girl's voice, quite loud and very clear, something about an old fuddy-duddy who was jealous because he was past it. A moment later Cutler caught him up.

'Cleared away?' Kemp asked sardonically.

'Cleared away?'

Kemp said, 'The young woman.'

14

'Oh – yes, sir, Commodore, I guess so. All aboard, I told her
... and stand well clear of the bubble-gum chutes.'

'What?'

'US Navy pipe, sir. Boats' crews keep out from under the
chewed gobs coming down the chute – '

'This isn't the US Navy, Cutler. Do you chew gum?'

'Why, yes, sir, Commodore, I guess I – '

'Not any more you don't.'

'Sir?'

'You heard.' Kemp's tone was harsher than he'd intended:
he'd once sat on some gum in a railway carriage. He believed
Cutler had taken umbrage; there was a hurt silence as they
embarked aboard the drifter to be greeted by Captain Theakston's upraised timepiece. That watch looked as though it might
have belonged to Theakston's grandfather; it had an uncompro-
mising Yorkshire aspect.

ii

Tex Cutler was one of the home-thinkers as the *Hardraw Falls*
dropped south towards Colonsay, but not of the USA: Oban
with the girl in residence was currently his idea of home, though
he doubted if he would ever see either again. The return convoy,
the QP out of Archangel – or if the freeze did in fact come sooner
than expected, then out of Murmansk – wasn't likely to sail for
Oban. More likely Liverpool, possibly the Clyde. Not that the
girl would be around anyway, of course. She was going back to
Glasgow, true, but only for a few days. She was fed up with the
Glasgow scene, the cold and the wet. The aunt would be back
soon and she was fed up with the aunt as well. Once you'd been
married, you didn't settle easily to aunts and their ways, however well-intentioned. She was heading back to London for a
while and after that God knew where. She might join the WAAF.
One thing was certain in Cutler's mind and that was that it
wouldn't be long before she found another serviceman passing
through and then she'd hitch her wagon to his temporary star.

Which was a pity. Cutler liked the girl a lot and wished he
could have stayed near to help her through. And he hoped she
wasn't going to get pregnant. . . .

'Cutler?'

'Yes, sir, Commodore?'

Kemp felt a twinge of irritation at being addressed as it were twice. 'I'd like the close-range weapons exercised before the hands stand down.' He paused. 'That's if it's all right with you, Captain Theakston?'

There was a brief nod. 'Aye. So long as there's no interference with the ship-handling in the firth.'

'There won't be. All right, Cutler, carry on, please.'

Cutler executed one of his salutes. 'Yes, sir, Commodore.'

Kemp said, 'That's not necessary, at night particularly – and not every time I open my mouth.'

'What's not – '

'The salute. Everything in its time and place, Cutler. Meanwhile, exercise close-range weapons.'

There was no Tannoy system aboard the *Hardraw Falls*: Cutler went to the bridge wing and shouted aft.

'Petty Officer of the close-range crews!'

The return shout came from the darkness. 'Here, sir.'

'What's your name, bloke?' Bloke was a term Cutler had picked up along the way, not realizing it was strictly an Australianism. Napper didn't like being called bloke in full hearing of junior ratings and he shouted back with a touch of truculence that his name was Petty Officer Napper.

'Okay. Report to the bridge, pronto.'

Pronto, was it? Petty Officer Napper moved for'ard at a fairly leisurely gait as befitted his rate and age. He climbed the starboard ladder and approached Cutler.

'Wanted me, sir?'

'Napper?'

'*Petty Officer* Napper, sir, yes.'

'Okay. Exercise action. All the way through from the word go. Get me? All guns' crews to fall out and go below and wait for the order, and I'll be timing how long it takes for all guns to be manned and ready to open fire – all right?'

'All right, sir, yes.' Napper's voice had a long-suffering backing to it. 'No Tannoy, sir. Going to press the tit, sir, sound the action alarm, are you, sir?'

It was Theakston who answered. 'No, he's not. Do that when there's no call for it, and what happens when an attack comes? I'll have no crying wolf aboard my ship.'

16

'But, sir, Captain Theakston – '

'I've nowt more to say and that's final.'

Kemp listened but didn't interfere. He was intrigued to know how Cutler would handle this. He hadn't long to wait. Cutler said, 'Okay. Petty Officer Napper'll be the alarm. All right, Napper?'

Napper's mouth fell open. 'Me, sir?'

'Yes. Stand by somewhere near the guns' crews' quarters. When I'm ready I'll pass the order down to you, exercise action, all right? When you get that, why, you just holler.'

There was an indeterminate sound from Petty Officer Napper. Kemp turned away, hiding a grin. Napper hadn't liked it and Kemp could appreciate his feelings but it showed one thing, and that was that Cutler could think on his feet. An assistant who could come up with something fast was welcome enough to Kemp. Improvisation was an essential attribute in anyone who went to sea but it wasn't often found among the inexperienced. Kemp paced the bridge, scanning the convoy and escorts through his binoculars, the dark, unlit shapes standing out in the loom from the water, and kept his ears cocked for Cutler's orders and the 'holler' from Petty Officer Napper. The resulting exercise was good in patches: the gunnery rates hadn't exercised together before and the turn-out wasn't as fast as Kemp would have liked, but once again he didn't interfere. He liked to trust his officers and there was something about Cutler that said he could take charge. He did, and in the process he made rings round Napper, who largely stood about with a look of bewilderment. It was plain to Kemp that Cutler knew his gun drill, at any rate so far as the close-range weapons side of it was concerned, and aboard the *Hardraw Falls* that was what counted.

iii

As the convoy made the turn off the Dubh Artach light and headed up for the Minch the wind came. A bitter wind from the north, from Iceland and the Arctic wastes, funnelling down on the ships between Tiree and Mull. The convoy altered again when Skerryvore was abeam to starboard, to head up between Barra and Rhum, and then they met the blow head on. The bows dipped to a roughening sea and, with the guns' crews by this time stood down, Petty Officer Napper turned into his bunk after rubbing some camphorated oil on his chest, now shrouded in a woollen scarf pulled tight about his ribs. Napper would have liked to strangle the drafting jaunty down in Pompey barracks, and a certain surgeon lieutenant as well. Napper had reported to the sick bay when he'd got his draft chit, spinning a yarn about vague pains here and there, principally in his chest. The sick bay tiffy had passed him on to the doctor because he'd insisted, and the doctor hadn't been interested beyond a brief bit of play-acting with a stethoscope, after which he'd said Napper was as fit as a fiddle, which Napper knew was a load of codswallop and proved the doctor, like all seagoing doctors, didn't know his job. To have said as much would have been to chance his arm too far, so he had to put up with it and now look where he was: Russia-bound with a dickey chest, the sods, a chest made worse by having to hang about in the open and bloody holler. Strike a light, Napper thought, Yanks!

Napper thought about home. The missus would be worried about him: she knew all about his chest. He wasn't too worried about her; home was in a Hampshire village behind Portsdown Hill, far enough away from Pompey and Gosport to be safe, nothing nearby to attract the Nazi bombers. Napper was more inclined to worry about his daughter, who at nineteen was man mad, go out with anything in uniform, even airmen. Marleen was a constant worry, liable at any moment to get a bun in the oven and destroy Napper's respectability. At his age, it wasn't fair.

Napper's last leave stuck in his mind like a bad go of tooth-ache. On his last night, Marleen had announced she was catching the bus into Pompey. There was a dance at Clarence Pier.

'Not on your nelly,' Napper had said.

'Why not?'

'Cos I say so.'

Marleen's nostrils had flared and her mother had made a bid to defuse the situation. 'It's not just that. Your dad's worried about the bombs.'

'What bombs?'

'Oh, for God's sake,' Napper said wearily. 'Don't you know there's a war on? It's me last night, too. Anyway, you're not going, so that's that.' He took up a poker and thrust angrily at the fire, or what there was of it. The Napper household was a patriotic one, even in the bath: like the King in Buckingham Palace, they never exceeded four inches of hot water.

'I *am* going! I'm bloody *going* so there!' A foot was stamped and Marleen's eyes flashed. 'I'm meeting Danny – '

'Not that wet weekend – '

'I don't care what you say. You never say anything good about any of my boyfriends – '

'That's cos there's nothing good to say.'

'Oh! You – you – ' Words had seemed to fail Marleen after that; there was too much head of steam inside. She whirled about and stormed out of the parlour, slamming the door with a crash that shook the whole house. A second later the door opened again and Marleen delivered her parting shot: *'Go and get stuffed, you rotten old fool!'*

Old fool eh? Napper could hear the shrill yell still. When Marleen had gone he'd stormed about the room, he remembered, talking about a taste of the belt when she got back, but Ethel had gone to Marleen's defence, saying that if he laid a hand on her she would walk out of the house. In the end he'd calmed down, though the scene had had an effect on his stomach and he felt quite sick and had to go to bed with some milk of magnesia and two aspirins, and even then hadn't slept a wink, lying there beside an unresponsive Ethel waiting for the sounds of Marleen's return and fearing the worst, not just the possibility of bombs but also Danny, even though he doubted if Danny was capable of putting a bun in anyone's oven. Thinking back now from somewhere north of Rhum, Napper began to sweat. At first he thought it was the effect of his own thoughts and bitter memories but after a while realized that it was the tightness of the wound scarf and too liberal a hand with the camphorated oil that was making his vest stick.

iv

By 1600 hours next day the convoy had left Cape Wrath on its starboard quarter and was heading into what had become a full gale. Out now from the narrows, out from the land's shelter,

19

they moved into the danger zone that stood between Cape Wrath and their Iceland landfall, as yet some two days' steaming ahead. The convoy was now larger: two ammunition ships had joined out of Loch Ewe, tagging on astern of the centre column after an exchange of signals with the senior officer of the escort and the Commodore. The ships moved on into the night and the gathering storm, their fo'c'sles swept by the heavy seas that dropped back aft to swill over the hatches and against the midship superstructures, pouring in white cascades from the hawsepipes and washports while the wind sang through the steel-wire rigging and buffeted the watchkeepers. No weather for U-boats; but Hitler had other methods and the first alarm came early next day as the morning watchmen were about to be relieved. Leading Signalman Corrigan made the report to Captain Theakston, wedged in a corner of the wheelhouse, grey with lack of sleep.

'Senior officer calling, sir. Aircraft bearing green two oh, hostile, closing.'

Theakston spoke to the officer of the watch. 'Call the Commodore, Mr Amory.' As he spoke he moved across the wheelhouse and brought a heavy hand down on the action alarm.

THREE

'Unexpected,' Kemp said. Up to now, the Luftwaffe had left the PQs alone, as he remarked to Theakston.

Theakston gave him a sideways look. 'There's always a first time,' he stated flatly. Kemp scanned the skies, which were a clear blue with a scud of white cloud racing before the wind. The attacking aircraft were at first hard to pick up; they were coming out of the sunrise. The cruiser *Nottingham*, away to starboard, was already in action, her ack-ack sending up shells that burst in puffs of smoke to dot the sky. Soon the Germans were in sight from the *Hardraw Falls*, keeping high, sweeping right over the convoy before coming back in for their bombing run.

'Buggers are well out of range,' Kemp said, referring to their height.

'Aye, they are that.' Captain Theakston was phlegmatic, almost indifferent. You did what you could, you handled your ship in accordance with your training and experience, and you hoped for the best. No use worrying. If you got hit, you got hit and that was all about it. Aboard the *Hardraw Falls* you'd go fast enough if you did get hit, blown straight up into the heavens to sit somewhere on God's right hand and look down on it all happening.

All the ships of the escort were firing now, all except those of the A/s screen who were forming the guard against U-boats and whose depth-charges would be vulnerable in the racks and throwers. The sky above the convoy seemed filled with the shell bursts, a shrapnel curtain to keep the attack high and hinder the bomb-aimers.

'Here they come,' Kemp said suddenly. 'Laying eggs. . . .'

They watched as the bombs dropped from the bays, clusters of them that spread wider as they fell. The sea became dappled with waterspouts. A ragged cheer went up from the decks of the Commodore's ship as the convoy steamed on unscathed: not one hit. The next bombing run came in at reduced height, the Germans taking a chance on the ack-ack fire, zooming across with a roar of engines and this time to better effect: three ships, two in the port column and one in the starboard, were hit. Those in the port column, not badly damaged apparently, moved on. The starboard one had carried a cargo of cased oil and had taken a bomb on her fore hatch. There was a brilliant flash and a spreading column of smoke that spiralled and billowed for hundreds of feet into the sky. More explosions came, and more thick, oily smoke, as the fire took charge below and the shattered ship settled lower in the water.

'Not many'll come out of that,' Theakston said in a flat voice. There was no response from the Commodore: these were the times that Kemp detested with every part of his mind. A seaman's instinct was to stop and help, and all he could do was to steam on and make sure that all the other ships steamed on as well. The overall business of the war came first, and you didn't hazard more cargoes and more lives in the middle of an attack. But it still left a nasty taste and a certain knowledge that however long your life lasted there would be no forgetting.

This time, it was to be pointed up cruelly.

Leading Signalman Corrigan reported. 'Signal from ss *Wicksteed Park*, sir – request permission to stand by for any survivors.' Corrigan added, '*Wicksteed Park*'s next astern of the one that went up, sir.'

'Yes. Answer: "You are not repeat not to stop engines but may lower nets".'

'Aye, aye, sir.' Corrigan flashed the answer with his Aldis, voice and face expressionless. Kemp wondered what he was thinking – probably the same as himself: that in such desperately cold sea, men would die within the minute, that to lower nets and hope to catch anything would be as forlorn as looking for a sixpence in the Sahara? Just a sop to Kemp's own conscience, better than a flat refusal order. A ship sweeping past, the shocked survivors, if any were alive, too dazed and broken to reach out a hand for the trailing nets – he might just as well have sent that refusal.

Cutler was on the bridge now, come up from aft where he'd been with the close-range weapons above the after island, yelling words of encouragement as the gunners pumped away, sitting in their harness as the guns swivelled after the enemy to no effect.

Kemp faced him. 'I gave no order to open fire, Cutler.'

'No, sir.'

'You know the general order, given at the convoy conference: no firing from the merchant ships except when under individual attack or when aircraft are clearly within range.'

'Yes, sir, Commodore – '

'God damn it, the country's desperately short of all kinds of ammunition! So is the ship. We're going to need to make every round count. Remember that, all right?'

'Yes, sir. It was just that I wanted to have a crack at them, that's all.'

Kemp nodded, understanding only too well. 'All right, Cutler. Just bear in mind what I said. See that the order from the bridge is awaited in future.'

'Yes, sir, Commodore.' A hand started to go into one of Cutler's odd salutes, but wavered before its manoeuvre had been completed. Two minutes later the attack was broken off, very suddenly. Soon after that the reason became apparent: the RAF had arrived, presumably from Shetland.

Theakston said, 'Better late than never.'

ii

With just the one loss to report, the PQ convoy reached the shelter of Iceland and the anchors were let go in Hvalfiord. Shelter was not quite the word, except as regards the enemy: the wind was bitter, the cold intense. A naval motor-cutter came off to fetch the Commodore and his assistant and Mason Kemp made his report to the Naval Officer in Charge while the escort vessels and merchant ships topped up their fuel tanks for the long run to Archangel. The damage to the two ships, Kemp reported, was not enough for them to be taken out of the convoy provided the base had facilities to effect temporary repairs. This, NOIC said, would be attended to so far as possible in the time available.

'Can you delay our sailing if necessary?' Kemp asked.

NOIC shrugged. 'My scope for that is limited, Commodore. The Russians are said to be bellyaching for supplies ... but of course they won't be wanting a short delivery. There's another angle, though: we're not so far off the winter freeze-up around Archangel. It's going to come *early* this year, so the Met boys say now. An unexpected shift in the weather charts. You might get in, but you might not get out again after discharging cargo if we cut it too fine.'

'Murmansk instead?'

'Yes, we may have to ask the Russians to approve a re-routeing – you'll be kept informed while at sea, of course.' NOIC, a captain RN named Frobisher, seemed, Kemp thought, to have something else on his mind but if so was either keeping it to himself or hadn't yet got around to it. Frobisher asked abruptly, 'Gin?'

'Thank you. Just a small one.'

'That's all you'll get. It's not easy to keep Iceland properly supplied with all the essentials! You don't know how lucky you are to have a sea appointment.'

Kemp smiled politely but was thinking of the ship that had blown up. Lucky to be at sea? Perhaps the dead had thought so too, until they'd stopped thinking altogether in the instant of disintegration. But Frobisher, whilst pouring two small gins with plain water, was speaking again. . . .

'I'm sorry,' Kemp said. 'My thoughts were – somewhere else. I'm not convinced that there's much luck about the sea. Not for some.'

Forbisher looked at him keenly. 'Yes, I think I understand. That ship. Rotten – I know that. Goes against the grain, just leaving them to it. But there wouldn't have been many left – *any* left most likely.'

'I still hate my own guts.'

'Well – don't. You know perfectly well you had no choice. Here, drink this.' Frobisher put the gin glass in Kemp's hand. 'I can rake up another if you feel you need it, and you'll be more than welcome. And a word of advice if I may offer it: when you get back aboard, relax and have a bloody good skinful!'

24

'I've a damn good mind to,' Kemp said.

He did have a second gin and while he was drinking it NOIC relieved his mind of its burden.

iii

Returned aboard, Kemp went to his cabin, looking grim and upset. He poured himself a whisky: like any other ship, naval or merchant service, the *Hardraw Falls* carried a plentiful supply of spirits and tobacco and Kemp had ordered cigarettes and a bottle of whisky from the chief steward's stores. The drink, a short one, poured, there was a tap at the door and Sub-Lieutenant Cutler came in.

'Well, Cutler?'

'Request, sir, Commodore – '

'I have one of my own, Cutler. A request.'

'Sir?'

Kemp said, 'Aboard a ship I may be God, but I'm not the Holy Trinity nor even the holy couple, if there is such a thing. Get me?'

'Why, no, sir, Commodore, not – '

'There you go again! I'm sir or I'm Commodore, but not both at once. Let's settle for the unadorned sir, shall we?'

'Why, sure, sir, Commodore . . . sir. If that's what you want.'

'I do. Like a whisky?'

'Thank you, sir.'

Kemp poured, the broad gold band on his cuff catching a shaft of sunlight striking through the scuttle. 'You had a request. What is it?'

'Not me personally, sir. Petty Officer Napper. To see the doctor ashore, if there is one. If not, then the doctor aboard the *Nottingham*, sir.'

'Reason?'

'Chest pains, sir. And a few more elsewhere.' Cutler paused. 'If I may offer an opinion, sir, I reckon Napper doesn't want to go to Russia.'

'No more do I, Sub. But you may be right. Whether you are or not, he'll have to be allowed to see the doctor. Make a signal to the Flag . . . ask for a medical appointment soonest possible.

25

Better ask them to send a boat, too. They've got more spare hands and boats than the *Hardraw Falls*.'

'Very good, sir.' Cutler finished the whisky. 'Sir, the orders from NOIC —'

'I have them in mind. I'll be talking to Captain Theakston shortly, Cutler. For now, keep the orders under your hat.'

'I'll do that thing, sir, Commodore ... sorry, sir.' Cutler left the cabin. Kemp went over to the square port beside his bunk and looked out across the fore well-deck and the battened-down cargo hatches to the shore beyond. Iceland in midwinter was a cheerless, grim place, snow and mostly iron-hard skies, rock-like mountains, sea-worn ships with rust marks drooling from the hawse-pipes and the engine-room outfall and along the sides, the odd small boat pushing through leaden water, and overall the terrible, biting cold made worse when the wind blew up. Turning away from a depressing scene, Kemp poured himself another whisky. NOIC had been right: one or two over the odds often helped when it was safe and prudent to take them, as it was now. The *Hardraw Falls* was not his responsibility and Theakston was well capable of dealing with anything that might arise in that direction. In port the Commodore was a spare number for most of the time.

The Commodore might as well enjoy his respite and kill the pain of memory. Kemp seldom drank alone but by this time he had ascertained that his initial belief had been correct: Captain Theakston was a teetotaller.

The whisky went down and he felt better. He had one more, a small one and the last, and was about to put the bottle back in the cupboard over his washbasin when there was another knock and Theakston came in.

iv

Petty Officer Napper disembarked on to the bottom platform of the flagship's port accommodation ladder and ascended to the quarterdeck, which he saluted punctiliously. A starchy looking lieutenant RN strode the deck complete with looped sword-belt straps of black patent leather dangling empty of any sword in in-

dication of his current duty as officer of the watch. He looked
Napper up and down, and Napper saluted again.

'Petty Officer Napper, sir, from *Hardraw Falls* to see the qu –
medical officer, sir.'

The lieutenant made no reply but lifted a hand to the corporal
of the gangway, a Royal Marine. Napper was taken in hand and
led by a sideboy along pipe-lined alleyways with corticened
decks, over coamings in the watertight sections, the well-
remembered ambience of a warship, not experienced for quite a
while; until his draft to the *Hardraw Falls*, Napper had served
ashore ever since his recall on mobilization in 1939, a nice soft
number in Pompey barracks as petty officer i/c cleanliness in the
seamen's blocks. It was a rotten shame he'd been propelled out
of it at his age.

He reached the sick bay: it was a funny thing but it was like
when you'd gone to the expense of buying a new washer and
when you came to fit it the bloody tap had stopped dripping . . .
the pains had gone from his chest. He gave a racking cough to
stir them up but without success. His long, mournful face
lengthened still further: the quack would go and say he was
swinging the lead, malingering, but he wouldn't say that if he
could only see Napper's stock of medicines aboard the *Hardraw
Falls*: if you were just a lead-swinger you didn't go to that sort of
expense, not on a PO's rate of pay. Stood to reason, did that. As
he waited for the quack he felt a little twinge in his chest
and hope returned, but not for long. In the first place he was
seen by a surgeon lieutenant, which was a disappointment.
As, in a sense, a guest patient from a merchant ship he'd
expected the surgeon commander. No such luck, and the
surgeon lieutenant was brief and preoccupied. Preoccupied
with bugger all, Napper thought, naval quacks hadn't much to
do normally.

Napper was told to remove his upper clothing.

'Been using camphorated oil,' the surgeon lieutenant
remarked.

'Yessir.'

'Quite a stench. Good stuff though, camphorated oil.'

'Yessir. I – '

The inevitable stethoscope interrupted Napper's discourse
but his time came when the quack asked what his symptoms had

27

been. There had been many and Napper detailed them at some length, interspersing them with nasty coughs.

'Yes, yes, I see. There's nothing to worry about, just a touch of fibrositis.'

'I smokes a lot, sir – '

'So do we all.' The quack's fingers, Napper had noticed, were yellow with nicotine. Napper, thinking he might as well make the most of his visit, began to go through his ailment list. He spoke of his bowels, which was a mistake brought on by nervousness and the feeling that he was on a loser as usual. Given an opening on bowels, the quack cut him short, told him to get dressed and nodded at the leading sick-berth attendant, who seemed to understand without a word being said. When Napper was once again dressed, the LSBA handed him a glass of dark liquid.

He said unnecessarily, since Napper knew it of old, 'Black Draught, PO. Number Nines in liquid form you might say.'

Mutinously, Napper drank it up: bowel mixture! In the Andrew, so long as your bowels were regular, you were fighting fit. Regularity cured even chests.

v

Captain Theakston had seen the whisky bottle: Kemp had made no attempt to hide it, seeing no reason why he should act like a maiden caught being chastely kissed.

'I know you don't drink, Captain – but you'd be welcome enough to join me, of course.'

'Thank you, no. Life-long abstinence has suited me well enough. You were in the liners, of course.' Theakston said that as though the liners were the iniquitous jaws of hell, leading inevitably to the everlasting fires. In some respects that would have been a fair assessment, Kemp knew. Too much cheap liquor, too much time on one's hands, and always the temptations provided by the passengers. Women and drink: parties always going in the cabins, in the many bars, ship's officers very welcome. Many had fallen by the wayside and Theakston would be aware of this. There was a stiffness about the master's manner, more so than usual, and Kemp hoped he wasn't in for a sermon: Theakston had a somewhat pulpitish look about him. But it appeared that that was not his current mission. He said, 'Your visit to the shore, Commodore. I was wondering, are there any orders?'

'As a matter of fact, yes, there are. I was intending to tell you, Captain.' A grin came to Kemp's face along with a sudden wicked desire to shock. 'I'm afraid the bottle intervened briefly.'

'Aye. . . .'

That expressive face of Theakston's was off-putting: one look from the Captain of the *Hardraw Falls* was the equivalent of a speech in Parliament and much more to the point. Kemp knew he should not have given way to an impulse to tease; he felt almost as though he were back again to his apprentice days, hauled up before the master for some omission – or for smuggling a flask of whisky aboard. He had to rehabilitate himself somehow, not an easy task under the stare of Theakston's formidable eyes. Best leave it. . . .

He said, 'There's a special job for us, Captain.'

'For the *Hardraw Falls*, or for the convoy?'

'The *Hardraw Falls*. NOIC – '

'Because you're aboard, because my ship carries the Commodore?'

Straight to the point, like any Yorkshireman. Theakston hadn't come down with the last shower. Kemp said, 'Yes, that is so. We're to rendezvous with a British submarine coming south, round the North Cape from Murmansk – '

'Position?'

'68°10' north, 12°40' east. Off the Lofotens.'

'Close to the Norwegian coast. Too close.'

'It has to be accepted, Captain – '

'Is there a Norwegian involvement?'

Kemp nodded. 'Yes. The submarine will have picked up a man coming out in a fishing boat from the Norwegian coast north of the rendezvous position, too close inshore to divert a ship from the convoy safely – too close navigationally and as regards the Germans. The man is obviously regarded as important, and – '

'Do you know his identity, Commodore?'

Kemp hesitated for a moment, then said quietly, 'Yes, as it happens I do. I know him personally . . . that's why we've been landed with the job. He travelled frequently to and from Australia before the war, in my company's ships – '

'Do I take it he's British, not Norwegian – a British agent?'

Kemp said crisply, 'Neither. He's German. This is strictly between the two of us, Captain – us and Cutler. I'm under the strictest orders.'

Theakston nodded, his eyes never leaving Kemp's face. 'I understand. I'll ask one thing only: this man, this German – I take it he knows you are aboard the *Hardraw Falls* and because you have sailed together he trusts you, and has asked to be brought aboard to join you.'

Kemp gave a heavy sigh and shook his head. 'Wrong, Captain. He knows nothing of my appointment. *I*'ve been chosen by Whitehall because *they* know we'd become good friends – this man's pre-war business interests in Australia are known to Intelligence, and naturally, when asked, the company's London offices co-operated in making passenger lists, pre-war ones, available.'

'Yes, I see. Then – '

'When he boards, yes, he will know me, of course. That's going to be the hard part.'

Theakston looked at him critically for a few moments, then said, 'I'm going to make a guess or two. This German, now. For some reason he's to be landed in Archangel – else, they'd have waited for the QP homeward. Again for some reason – I'll not ask *what* in either case – he's to give you his trust. It's your job to encourage that.' When there was no response from Kemp, Theakston leaned forward and put a heavy hand on the Commodore's shoulder. 'And now I think I know the reason for the whisky bottle. And I don't blame you.'

vi

The facts were simple enough once a straight line was drawn through the intrigue and skulduggery that were part and parcel of the Intelligence services on both sides. Simple but dirty: again, part of Intelligence. NOIC hadn't liked it any more than Kemp, but the excuse was, of course, that the man was an enemy agent and nothing else could be allowed to count. Truth, decency, honesty were out for the duration. Kemp felt it was going to be like the massacre of Glencoe all over again, the hospitable MacDonalds as it were to fall again to the Campbell treachery. He remembered Gunther von Hagen very well indeed, had always been pleased to see his name in the passenger list, had always, once he'd gained command as master, had the German seated at his table in the saloon. Many an after-dinner drink they'd taken together in his quarters. Von Hagen was a chess player, so was Kemp, and they had been of about equal standard. Von Hagen had worked for a firm of London wool importers, and had much business at the Australian end. It seemed that shortly before the outbreak of war von Hagen had returned to his country and had been co-opted into German Military Intelligence, in which he was now a colonel. His sphere of operations, NOIC had told Kemp, had been Norway – digging out the Resistance groups, a dirty game certainly, but he had never so far as was known operated against the British themselves. Kemp had been able to confirm that von Hagen, at any rate before the war, had been very much an Anglophile and had felt at home in England.

Kemp also knew that the German's *bête noir* had been the Russians. Communism he had detested; he and Kemp had had many discussions as to the way the world had been going. Kemp had never concealed his own hatred of the Nazis and their regime, but von Hagen had been non-committal; he was, Kemp believed, a Nazi but a lukewarm one, one who merely accepted rather than fully supported, except as regards his loathing of communists. But all that was unimportant now. Von Hagen had done his duty, NOIC had said, quoting British Intelligence, and had done well – or bloodily – in Norway. That was, until he'd slipped up and had been taken prisoner by the Resistance, who were now handing him over to the British.

Or so he believed. In fact he was to be taken on to Russia once the transfer from the submarine had been made. In Archangel he was to be handed over to the security police: the men in the Kremlin had a use for his knowledge of Norway and the German defences there. Kemp's job was the simple part: he was under orders to talk to an old friend and find out all he could about German Intelligence, on a basis of the old pals' act, before von Hagen was handed over to whatever awaited him after his interrogation by the Russians: probably Siberia, possibly death. His lever was to be a promise that von Hagen would not in fact be handed over to the Russians. A promise that was not to be kept.

No job for a convoy Commodore; but the orders had been very strict and were to be carried out to the letter. No jiggery-pokery on Kemp's part, no back-tracking for an old friend. Whitehall had no wish to upset the Kremlin.

FOUR

So now Iceland lay behind as the PQ convoy headed on its course for the rendezvous behind the busily sweeping A/S screen. The commanding officers of the escorting warships had been put in the picture only to the extent of being informed at the departure conference of the British submarine's presence ahead of the convoy, and this had added a new dimension of danger: the submarine would proceed on the surface whenever possible but might have to submerge at any time; no Asdic contacts in the relevant area were to be attacked until the identity had been positively established, which in effect meant that no contacts at all could be attacked whilst submerged. The submarine's human cargo was not to be put at risk.

The senior officer of the escort, Rear-Admiral Fellowes, had been informed in Hvalfiord of the full facts, the only one apart from Kemp who had, and he had been livid. 'It's damn lunacy! Putting the whole convoy at risk for a blasted Nazi! Who the hell dreamed this one up, can you tell me that?'

NOIC had shrugged. 'It comes from high up, I believe, sir. But enough said – I can't exceed my brief or my guts'll go for garters.'

'I'd like someone's guts laid bare,' Fellowes said in a voice like ice. 'I'll tell you one thing – I'll be putting my representations to Their Lordships in very plain language once this is over. Too late, I know – but good for the blood pressure just to have it to look forward to!'

ii

Kemp, who normally liked to take a ship's company into his confidence when it was safe to do so, letting them know the risks and chances, knew that this time it would not be safe even if the orders for silence had not been so rigid. At any moment the convoy could come under attack, the Commodore's ship could be sunk, conceivably some men could be picked up by a U-boat or a German destroyer – unlikely perhaps but the possibility couldn't be disregarded – and they might be made to talk. The presence off Norway of the submarine must not become known. So nothing at all was said; even so, by some curious alchemy of ship life, it was known even before the *Hardraw Falls* had cleared away from Hvalfiord that something was in the wind and that this was no ordinary Russian convoy.

As so often happened aboard ship, the source had been the Captain's steward, a plump man named Torrence who reckoned he could tell from Theakston's mood what the future held. Not just Theakston – any captain, and that included Commodore Kemp, upon whom also he was attending. Little bits of preoccupation, a show of irritation over trifles, the gesture of a hand and the expression of a face, they all told their story to Torrence, who was a great putter together of two and two.

'Something up,' he remarked to the chief steward in the latter's office.

Buckle cocked an eye at him. 'Oh, yes, and what, may I ask?'

'Don't know that, not yet. But Kemp ... he came back from the shore looking pretty sick. Had some nasty news I reckon, Chief.' Torrence wiped the back of a hand across his nose. 'Went on the bottle an' all.'

'Measured, did you?'

'I always keeps a check.'

Buckle nodded; it was a steward's duty to see that an officer's stock was kept up, not an onerous duty in the case of Captain Theakston, but Buckle also knew that Torrence was not above helping himself to the odd tot, a steward's perks in Torrence's view. He asked sardonically, 'How much, eh?'

'Not a lot, but enough, seeing as it was morning.'

'Doesn't signify. . . .'

'Not on its own, no, maybe not. But when the Old Man come out of Kemp's cabin ... well, *he* looked sick an' all and got stuck into me just because there was a speck of dust on his desk. Relieving his feelings, like.'

34

'So what's your deduction, eh?'

Torrence blew out his cheeks and looked like a pale pink balloon. 'Dunno. Early to say. But if I might hazard a guess, like ... I reckon Kemp was given word of the bloody Jerries being out in strength.'

Buckle rubbed reflectively at his jaw and looked at Torrence through narrowed eyes. Torrence often had the buzz dead to rights and that was a fact not to be disregarded. A kind of clairvoyance, or more likely a big ear to the keyhole. Thoughts of the cargo beneath the hatches went through Buckle's mind: they were all sitting on sudden death. You didn't usually think much about it, you got used to it, and if you did think too much you'd go round the bend sharpish. You always hoped for the best, confident that it wasn't you that was going to get it. All the same, it was human nature to be curious, which was why the buzz-mongers always had an avid audience. This time, Torrence's buzz wasn't all that much.

Buckle said, 'That wouldn't be news, would it?' He pursed his lips as a sudden thought struck. 'Think it's anything to do with that Yank?'

'Cutler? Maybe it is but I dunno yet.'

Torrence went about his business, which currently was seeing to Theakston's and Kemp's laundry, also Cutler's: Torrence, accustomed to wait upon the master only, was now a busy man, as busy as the steward who attended on the other deck officers single-handed. Buckle sat on at his desk, staring at a calendar depicting a frozen-looking semi-nude girl against a backdrop of December snow with compliments of one of the ship's suppliers. Buckle stared without seeing. That American. Canadian uniform, odd in itself. He knew Cutler wasn't a Canadian: the Texas accent was unmistakable. For a period of his life Buckle had served in a tanker that made frequent use of the port of Galveston on the Gulf of Mexico and he'd known many Texans. So why an American – an American on the Commodore's staff of all things?

It could tie up.

Some US angle, but what?

Buckle felt a prickle of fear run up and down his spine: there was the tang of special operations, and such could mean extra danger. Special operations, and the destination Russia. Buckle, a divorced man who had not remarried, thought of his mother, a widow living alone in Bermondsey. If anything happened to him, it would be curtains for the old lady. He was her life, and now he was moving towards some US conspiracy with the Russians, and the States not yet even in the war themselves.

Not yet.

The day was 7 December; and next morning's BBC News brought the word to the *Hardraw Falls* and the world at large that the Japanese had shattered the United States Pacific Fleet at Pearl Harbor.

iii

'Bastards!' Tex Cutler spoke through clenched teeth, his face white with shock. Two waves of aircraft, a total of forty torpedo-bombers, a hundred high-level bombers, a hundred and thirty dive-bombers, escorted by around eighty fighter aircraft. *Arizona, Oklahoma, West Virginia, California* – all gone. The *Tennessee* and the *Nevada* had been put out of commission. That was the big stuff and it wasn't the full tally. There were tears in Cutler's eyes.

Kemp put a hand on his shoulder. 'I'm desperately sorry, Cutler.'

'All those ships. Jesus, I lived for the Navy! If we'd gone into the war sooner, I'd have joined.'

'And I'd have lost a good officer. I'm glad I didn't, Cutler, very glad.'

'So I'm glad you're glad.' Cutler spoke with an intense fierceness, staring unseeingly across the cold grey of the sea.

Kemp said, 'Go below to my cabin, Cutler. You'll find whisky in the cupboard. Help yourself.'

Cutler seemed to take a grip. He said, 'Thanks, sir. I guess I feel like getting stewed.'

'Don't overdo it.'

Cutler went below. In the Commodore's cabin he found Torrence, who was polishing around. Torrence said, 'Good morning, sir.'

'The Commodore's Scotch, and fast.'

'Coming right up, sir.' Torrence went to the cupboard and brought out the bottle. 'Bad news on the wireless, sir.'

'Right.'

Torrence shoved his polishing cloth into his trouser pocket, from which it dangled like a yellow pennant. 'Reckon the US'll have to come in now, sir.' There was something of a gloat in his voice.

Cutler stared at him, a reddish fleck in his eyes. 'Fuck off,' he said tightly. 'Just for Christ's sake fuck off out of it.'

iv

Two days later, by which time the convoy was not so far off the rendezvous position and steaming unattacked through bitter but calm seas, the BBC brought more news: Germany and Italy had declared war on the United States. The feeling throughout the *Hardraw Falls* was one of relief tinged with guilt: America had proved a good friend short of actual war and it was not up to British seamen to wish the agony of war upon her, but the fact that America and Britain would henceforward stand together was immensely heartening.

According to Petty Officer Napper, Adolf Hitler would now be wetting his pants in large quantities. 'Have the bugger on the run soon,' he said with satisfaction to Leading Signalman Corrigan.

'Well, let's hope so, PO. He's far from finished yet.'

'Ho! Know so, do you?'

'No.'

'Then don't shoot your mouth orf, son. Think of all those Yankee troops that'll be coming over any minute!'

'Poor sods. Why should they pull our chestnuts out of the fire?'

Napper glared. 'That's a fine thing to say! We're all white, aren't we?'

'So's Hitler – Aryan white. So's Musso, so's Stalin . . . what's colour got to do with it, PO?'

Napper knew Corrigan was a superior bugger. Angrily he said, 'Don't be bloody cheeky, all right? I just don't like blacks, that's all.' He turned and walked aft along the well-deck, past the after hatches towards the superstructure above the engine-room and the engineers' accommodation, realizing he'd said something daft that would make Corrigan even more superior in his attitude. There was something about Corrigan that made Napper say daft things; he'd tried to be matey since Corrigan was not only something of a medic but also a leading hand and those in authority had to stick together. But maybe that had been a mistake: Corrigan's lofty tones were reacting on his state of health and the chest pains had returned to plague him, together with a vague unrest in his stomach, a churning feel. He wished he could diagnose it, but wishing was vain, and in fact Corrigan hadn't been much help. Napper thought of the seaman's bible, the Admiralty Seamanship Manual: by rights there ought to be an issue to all hands of an Admiralty Medical Manual, then they'd all know what was up with them and be able to keep a check on the quack.

Petty Officer Napper had his own checks to make, on the ship's armament. He'd done his stuff on the bridge and monkey's island before encountering Corrigan; now he climbed the ladder to go through the drill on the close-range weapons mounted on the after superstructure, first chivvying the AB sitting in the straps and dreaming of home. Or looking as if he was. And half-frozen with it.

'Come on then, lad.'

Able-Seaman Grove looked round. 'Come on where, PO?'

'Bloody look lively!' Napper snapped.

'How?' Grove looked blank.

'Don't give me any lip, lad. I said, look lively, look as if you *belonged*.'

Napper, in Grove's view, was a right old tit, a dug-out from very deep down who even now hadn't yet quite surfaced. What Napper knew about modern weapons could be written on a half-farthing. And what the sod did 'look lively' mean when you were all ready at your gun and all that was missing was the enemy? Grove had a sudden impulse: he gripped the gun, swung it in a circle and made loud phut-phut noises at imaginary Nazi aircraft swooping in from all directions.

Napper stared, his long grey face reddening. 'What's all that in aid of? Going round the bend, are you? Or being bloody cheeky?'

'No, PO. Looking lively, that's all. Dealing with the Luftwaffe – '

'That's enough o' that, sonny boy. Moment you come orf

watch, you'll be on the bridge, one-one-two, up before Mr Cutler, all right?'

'You putting me in the rattle, PO?'

'Got it in one. Charged with insolence to your superior officer.' Napper turned away, seething and feeling more unwell than ever, his check on the rest of the after close-range weapons left undone. As his cap disappeared down the ladder Grove made a rude gesture towards where he had been standing. The PO was totally impossible: nag, nag, nag. Maybe he was missing his sex life, but so were they all . . . and in point of fact, Grove reckoned, Napper didn't get any anyway. He didn't look the sort: to Napper, the word 'fanny' would mean nothing more than a mess kettle.

v

Still ahead of the PQ convoy, the pick-up submarine had remained submerged as close in to the Norwegian coast as was navigationally possible. Now, under cover of the darkness, she had come to the surface. With his navigator and a signalman the lieutenant in command scanned the surrounding water through his binoculars. He was a shade early on his ETA as notified to the local Resistance command by a coded broadcast from London. No need for anxiety yet; but the tension was there already. Fortunately there was no moon: the sky was nicely overcast, the night pitch dark. But that wasn't a hundred per cent protection. The Nazis could be waiting: the Resistance had reported that there were no surface radar stations in this part of the coast so there were no worries on that score. But there could be other things: there could have been a leak. Even in the Resistance there were Quislings, and the man to be picked up wouldn't have been operating entirely on his own.

The minutes passed, agonizingly slow. The terrible cold encroached, penetrating duffel coats and oilskins, scarves, mittens and balaclavas. It was cold enough almost to freeze thought. The hills, the rocks of the coast, were aloom with snow and ice, making men aware of them even through the thick dark: high, impregnable, threatening.

They all knew they could have entered a trap.

The lieutenant turned as the scrape of feet was heard on the ladder leading up to the conning-tower. A voice said, 'Kye up, sir.'

'Keep your bloody voice down!' The Lieutenant spoke in a hiss.

'Sorry, sir.' A seaman emerged from the hatch, miraculously carrying a tin tray with three mugs of thick, sweet cocoa which he handed round. 'Not a drop spilt, sir.'

'Congratulations!'

'Watch out for cockroaches, sir.'

'If I find just one, you'll need to watch out for yourself.'

The man grinned and vanished back down the ladder to the boat's interior. The watch, the seemingly interminable wait, went on. The lieutenant looked continually at the luminous dial of his wrist-watch: he had a deadline after which he was under orders to extricate his submarine to sea. But there had been something underlying those orders: a hint that failure to bring off the German agent would make the submarine's co an unpopular officer in high Whitehall circles. A whiff of cigar smoke, perhaps . . . Mr Churchill was said to be often irrational and impetuous and blame didn't always end up in the right quarter. A lieutenant in command of a submarine was in no position to control the actions and movements of the Norwegian Resistance or to ensure the security of their communications. But to tell Mr Churchill that would be to risk personal disaster. The lieutenant, as the minutes ticked past towards the deadline, was on tenterhooks. A nasty decision was coming up. Did he obey orders and scarper out to sea? Or did he heed that hint, and hang on in defiance of the orders? Typical Admiralty, he thought. Whatever you did, they could have you by the short hairs. If blood, the lieutenant thought, was the price of Admiralty, then ambiguity was its watchword.

When it happened the suddenness caught them all on the hop and the lieutenant literally felt the pause in his heartbeat: a voice came from the darkness on the port quarter of the submarine.

'Captain, we are here.'

The lieutenant turned quickly. He could see nothing. No one had seen anything. There had been no sound, just nothing, no sound of oars or paddles, no swish of water. A moment later, as the lieutenant climbed down to the after casing, a hand appeared and made a grab for the triatic stay. A body heaved itself up, followed by another and then another. The lieutenant saw a black inflatable dinghy being held alongside.

'Thank God you got here,' he said, finding nothing else to say.

'Yes. God is good and is on our side – with a little help from us! A case of Schnapps carelessly left ... there is drunkenness in a certain German mess tonight, and tomorrow more than heads will be sore. But now you are in a hurry – '

'You can say that again!'

'Therefore I will stop.' The Norwegian was a big man, built like a bear and almost as hair-covered as to his face. He turned to the man who had come aboard behind him, a man with a revolver held against his spine by the other Norwegian behind again. 'Here is your cargo, Captain.'

The lieutenenat saw the outline of a tall man, slim and upright. He was aware of a heel click and a stiff bow. He asked, 'Colonel von Hagen?'

'At your service, Captain.' The English was faultless, no trace of an accent. Presumably his command of Norwegian was as good. A hand was extended and the German said, 'How d'you do.' As he spoke, the bear-like Resistance man smashed down hard on his wrist.

'There was no need for that,' the lieutenant said.

'Captain, that hand is not for shaking by us or you. It has killed ... innocent people, patriots. Remember that. Now we shall go. And God go with all of us.' He and his companion dropped back into the dinghy and moved away as soundlessly as they had come. The lieutenant nodded at an armed seaman who had followed him down from the conning-tower and the German was led for'ard towards a hatch in the casing, a hatch that was clipped down behind him as he descended. The moment this had been done the submarine moved out, her motors going dead slow.

'Cutler?'

'Sir?'

'How far to the rendezvous?'

Cutler had just taken a look at the chart and had the answer ready. 'Seventy miles, sir.'

'Five hours' steaming,' Kemp said. 'Let's hope that submarine's on time. I don't want to have to hang about. Nor will the Rear-Admiral.'

'Out of our control, sir.'

'I know.' Kemp turned and paced the bridge wing, backwards and forwards, feeling caged – or feeling that he might become caged in a sense if he had to lie without way on the ship, or had to steam around in circles, waiting for the submarine to show. The German U-boats loved such a situation, and if a contact was found by the A/S screen there would be nothing they could do about it immediately in case it was the pick-up. In any case, if the wait was a long one, Kemp was going to endure it almost on his own. That had been thrashed out back in Hvalfiord: Kemp would not risk the main convoy. If the submarine was thirty minutes late he would fall out in company with one destroyer while the convoy steamed on, leaving him to catch up later. If the distance was great, then the chief engineer of the *Hardraw Falls* was going to have to give him everything he'd got in the way of power. The nearer they approached the North Cape, the greater would become the danger of attack. It would not be possible to reduce the convoy's speed, and never mind that it would be the Commodore who was arse-end Charlie. But all this was speculation, the crossing of bridges in advance that was a vital part of a commodore's job so that one was not caught with one's pants down. With any luck that submarine would be dead on time and dead in position. If she was not . . . like the submarine CO, Kemp had been aware of the pressures, the unspoken urgings of Whitehall, and he, too, would face dilemma: did he give it so long, and then chase up the convoy? Or did he risk the men aboard the *Hardraw Falls*, and wait? Again there was the similarity: any convoy commodore who frustrated the will of the Prime Minister would soon find himself on the beach.

As he paced, Kemp became aware of Petty Officer Napper

approaching Cutler together with a rating from the guns' crews. The rating had a mutinous look: Kemp kept his distance when he heard Napper say, 'Defaulter, sir. Will you see him, sir, please?'

Some niggling trouble. Napper was a real old woman. But of course discipline had to be maintained. Once again, Kemp wondered how Cutler would handle it.

Cutler said, 'Oh, Jesus. Yes, all right, Napper.'

'Thank you, sir.' There was a pause then Napper's nagging voice. 'Off cap! Able Seaman Grove, sir, official number P/JX 004399 . . . was insolent towards his superior officer, to wit, myself, sir, in that he – '

'You representing your own case yourself, Napper?'

'The ship, being a merchant ship, sir, has no regulating staff as such. Just me, as you – '

'All right, all right. Well? What are the grounds?'

Napper said, 'Made daft noises, sir. Phut-phut-phut, like. Shooting at imaginary aircraft, sir. After I'd give 'im an order.'

'What order?'

'To look lively, sir. 'Is response was like I said. Phut-phut-phut.'

'Aha.' Cutler kept a straight face. 'How many phuts?'

'How many – ?' Napper's face was scandalized: he was having the mickey taken. He said stiffly, 'Didn't count, sir.'

'*Didn't count?* Well, never mind, perhaps it's not all that important.' Cutler turned to Grove. 'What have you to say, Grove?'

'Nothing, sir.'

'Nothing? Then you admit the charge?'

'Yessir. Or rather no, sir. I was obeying orders.'

'To look lively?'

'That's right, sir. On'y way I saw of doing it.'

'Yes, I see. Don't do it again, Grove, or you'll be in trouble. No one's going to put up with insolent behaviour. So watch it, all right?'

'Yessir, thank you, sir.'

'Don't thank me, you've had a ticking off. Case dismissed.'

Napper looked as though he couldn't believe his ears. His eyes almost popped from his face and his mouth opened. But he met Cutler's cool stare and shut it again. He shouted, 'On cap!

43

Salute the officer! 'Bout turn – double march! Down the bleedin' ladder.'

Grinning, Cutler moved to the extremity of the bridge wing and joined Kemp. 'Did I do right, sir?'

'Yes, very right. I'd have done the same myself.'

'Napper's not pleased, sir. He wanted Commodore's Report.'

'Yes. Petty Officer Napper ... a word of advice, young Cutler: use his rate when speaking to him in front of junior ratings. It's only his due.'

Cutler said, 'Okay, sir.' Then, looking past the Commodore towards the van of the convoy, he stiffened. 'Flag's calling up, sir.'

Kemp turned. The signalman on watch was reading off the flashing light. He began calling out as he read. 'Commodore from Flag, sir: "RDF contact two surface vessels bearing red four five. Am investigating."'

Kemp saw the flagship heel over to port and increase speed even as the signal was coming through. 'RDF's a handy thing to have,' he said. 'One day, perhaps the merchant ships'll be fitted with it.'

Cutler asked, 'Think the enemy's out, sir?'

'I've no idea but I'll take no chances.' Kemp turned to the signalman, 'Pass the bearing to all ships by flag hoist.' He took up his binoculars. *Nottingham* was coming up now to her maximum speed of thirty-two knots and was being followed by the second cruiser now threading through the convoy columns on a dash across from her steaming position on the starboard beam. Ten minutes later the flagship signalled again across the widening gap of water: 'Two enemy destroyers in sight.'

Almost on the heels of the signal the *Nottingham* and the *Neath* had engaged. The sound of the big guns rolled back on the wind and Kemp saw the distant orange flashes and the smoke as the eight-inch batteries opened.

FIVE

The voice-pipe from the engine-room whistled in the wheel-house and Captain Theakston answered. 'Bridge, Captain speaking.'

'Chief here, Captain. What's up?'

'Enemy destroyers ahead. Two of them.'

'What are we going to do?'

'The convoy's opening formation. Stand by for engine altera-tions. And maybe bumps.' Theakston banged down the voice-pipe cover and concentrated on handling his ship. He'd seen bumps, and more than bumps, when a convoy was changing its formation – or barging freely about the ocean would often have been a more apt description. Kemp had a similar anxiety. Ships of different sizes and shapes and speeds, each with its own handling characteristics in the way it answered its helm – it was a far cry from warships of a single class responding to fleet ma-noeuvres on the executive from the Flag, carrying out red turns, white turns, blue turns, the colour being the indication of the particular manoeuvre to be carried out . . . currently it would be a case of each ship for itself and never mind the rule of the road. Kemp, who had had no option but to spread the ships out so far as possible – short of an actual scatter order, which might be given under much heavier attack – so as to disperse the target, felt like shutting his eyes and asking Cutler to tell him when something hit. The *Hardraw Falls* was maintaining her own course and speed, acting as some kind of lode star while the others altered around her, but Theakston was having to watch it pretty carefully. When a ship came slap across his bows, Theak-ston caused a flurry in the engine-room: the telegraph rang down for emergency full astern and Mr Sparrow, chief engineer, gritted his teeth hard. Engines never liked going from full ahead to full astern without a pause in between, but the bridge had spoken and that was that. The engine-room shook and shuddered and the plating of the starting platform, where Sparrow was standing, vibrated beneath his feet. He used his imagination as to what was going on up top : some silly bugger getting in their way and any moment they might be in collision. Then the engines were eased and put ahead again.

Sparrow let out a long breath of relief. It was cold outside and he didn't want to know, didn't want the cold to come through broken plates into his engine-room, nor seawater either. Sparrow didn't like the sea, not after thirty-odd years of it. He'd spent much of those thirty years wishing he hadn't gone to sea at all. It was an unsettling life, here today and gone tomorrow, and not overpaid although there were the perks of duty-free fags and whisky plus free living and a steward to wait on you. It had been all right when he was a younger man, in fact it had been fine, but not after he'd got married. By that time it was hard to find a job ashore ; he'd become too set in the ways of a ship's engineer and then he'd come up for chief and had settled for it. He would never have got an equivalent status anywhere other than aboard a ship.

He was joined on the starting platform by his second engineer, Bob Weller, who gave him what Sparrow considered a careful look as he did each time they came into contact. Sparrow knew why : Weller was next in seniority for chief of one of the Bricker Dockett Line's ships and Sparrow was getting long in the tooth, although he still had two years to go to retirement – unless the war went on that long and kept him at it. Bob Weller was impatient for promotion, and a man of Sparrow's age might well kick the bucket at any time, so Weller was always on the lookout for signs of illness, like a stroke or a heart malfunction. Mr Sparrow knew this perfectly well and occasionally played up. He did this time.

'Sudden flaps,' he said, sounding breathless. 'Don't like 'em.'

'Don't blame you, Chief.'

'Flutters the heart.' They were having to shout over the engine sounds, and Sparrow, for the sake of ageing bones, was hanging on tight as the *Hardraw Falls* rolled heavily to an alteration of course. The starting platform was a slippery place. Sparrow sometimes wondered if Weller sprayed oil on to the plates when he knew his chief would be down.

'You should take it easier, Chief.'

'Maybe I should.' Sparrow put a hand on his chest and managed to make his cheeks look hollow. He didn't miss the sudden look of hope in Weller's eye. There was no surer way to promotion than to have the chief engineer die at sea : the second stepped automatically into his shoes, at any rate for the rest of the voyage, and then with Weller's seniority it would be equally automatically confirmed on arrival back in UK. But Sparrow felt as fit as a fiddle and Weller was going to have a long wait yet.

ii

'*Nottingham* and *Neath* returning, sir !'

'Thank you, Corrigan.' Kemp, his binoculars levelled towards the port bow where the firing had been heard, had already seen the cruisers reappearing over the horizon. Once again a light was flashing from the Flag. Corrigan reported : 'Commodore from Flag, sir. "Interception successful. Both destroyers sunk. Have sustained superficial damage only." Message ends, sir.'

That was all : no indication of casualties, no indication of whether or not anyone had survived those terrible sea temperatures. Kemp said, 'Make to all ships, resume formation, course and speed.'

'Aye, aye, sir.'

Kemp looked at the clock on the wheelhouse bulkhead : an hour had passed, four more to go to the rendezvous. And the wind was increasing now, coming up to around Force Five on the Beaufort Scale, and it was filled with the threat of snow, bitterly cold and bringing the sea up in white horses that blew icily from the wave crests. Not bad enough to inhibit the operation of the U-boats, however ; and Kemp was surprised that no attack had developed. Of course there was plenty of time yet : the U-boats and surface vessels and aircraft could be waiting for the convoy to make its landfall off the North Cape, and come round it into the Barents Sea. Why cover the whole ruddy ocean, Kemp thought, when you knew the convoys had to close towards the

North Cape whatever happened, whatever their courses up from Scotland or Iceland?

With the ship now secured from action stations, Cutler came back from the after gun positions: the routine had to be gone through, the close-range weapons manned however useless they might be in some situations.

'All correct, Cutler?'

'All correct, sir, Commodore.'

Kemp clicked his tongue. 'You don't give up easily, Cutler.'

The American grinned tightly, more of a baring of teeth. 'My apologies, sir. Guess I'm thick at times. Or just a Yank.'

Kemp gave him a sharp look. 'You sound bitter.'

'Maybe I am. That Napper, he doesn't like Yanks.'

'He said so?'

'Sure he said so. Loud and clear – but not meant to be heard. Correction – meant to be heard but not meant to be addressed directly. If you get me, sir.'

Kemp grunted. 'Don't take it to heart, and don't hear – if *you* get *me*.'

'I get you all right, sir, and I agree. But I keep thinking of Pearl Harbor.'

'Of course you do. I think we all do, probably even Napper. But try to remember that the British Navy's been fighting the Atlantic war a long time now – '

'Not Napper. Not sitting on his ass in Portsmouth barracks till now. I'd like to have been there, to kick that ass of his all around the parade ground till he got prised loose – '

'All right, Cutler, I appreciate your feelings, but for God's sake and the convoy's don't let them show any more. You've let off steam. Let's leave it at that.'

'That an order?'

Kemp nodded briskly. 'It's an order, Cutler. I'm not having friction of that sort.'

'Yes, *sir*,' Cutler said, and tore off his weird salute, his face set. Then he turned about and went into the chartroom behind the wheelhouse. One of a commodore's assistant's jobs was to keep the chart corrections up to date on the Commodore's folio, and a whole batch of Notices to Mariners, incorporating the latest corrections, had come aboard in Hvalfiord. They would take time to enter in red ink on the relevant charts. But Kemp knew that

Cutler's main preoccupation currently was to keep out of range until he'd simmered down.

iii

By now the snow had started, thin so far, but the sky spoke of a really heavy fall to come. That sky was bleak, dark and heavy and foreboding as the day stretched into the afternoon. No sun at all, just that grey overcast and the spray being blown back over the bridge and wheelhouse and monkey's island, over the decks and the watchkeepers, over the reduced guns' crews of the watch, soaking into duffel coats and down the collars of oilskins to bring discomfort and piercing cold. Spindrift came, blown along the wind to search out every nook and cranny, and now the snow was blown with it, all the way, as it seemed, from the North Polar regions. The visibility was already coming down with the snow. Captain Theakston stood huddled in the port wing of the bridge, along with his chief officer, Amory. No use taking the easy way and keeping in the comparative warmth of the wheelhouse and trying to peer through the Kent clear-view screens as they whirled electrically at a speed that anyway in theory kept them clear of rain and snow. That was in Theakston's view the pansy way, the way that led to accidents in convoy. And because the master was on the bridge, Amory was also out in the open. The Old Man expected that and would have said so had Amory not come out into the biting cold. . . .

'You look frozen, Mr Amory.'

'I am frozen, sir.'

Theakston was sardonic. 'A little bit of snow! Come now. We don't complain about it in the North Riding, you know. Shepherds . . . do you think they aren't out in it continually, seeing to the sheep? Lambs get born in this sort of weather, in the dales.' Theakston flapped his arms about his body and his breath went like steam into the wind. 'You're a good chief officer, Mr Amory, but you'd make a poor shepherd, very poor.'

Amory laughed. 'I'm not much bothered about my qualities as a shepherd.' He looked around the convoy, at the warships of the escort, lean and hard but with their outlines blurred by the different shades of grey-blue of the camouflage paint, cutting through the waves with bones in their teeth and the water flinging back. The little ships of the A/s screen were having, as ever, the worst of it. Amory knew that those small ships were manned mainly by hostilities-only ratings and officered largely by the RNVR, what used to be called the Saturday-afternoon sailors until they'd proved themselves through two long, hard years of war at sea, never out of uniform, often enough watch on, stop on when the weather was bad or the enemy was out. And they and their mates in the cruisers and destroyers were the shepherds now, tending the convoys along the world's trade routes, keeping Britain fed, ensuring she and her allies were armed and supplied with troops. ... Theakston was going on about his favourite subject: Yorkshire and its dales and fells and great stretches of moorland. The road that wound through Wensleydale from Leyburn to Hawes, through the little villages, Wensley, West Witton, Aysgarth, Bainbridge, and off the main road the tiny, isolated communities of Thoralby, Thornton Rust, Stalling Busk, Countersett ... Amory had never seen any of them but he knew them intimately by now. There, Theakston said, was where the snow bit hard. You could be cut off for weeks, no movement except on horseback. And the winds blew strong too. Amory wondered why Theakston hadn't become a farmer instead of a seaman. There was, in fact, a lot of similarity between the two callings. Each was deeply committed to facing the weather in all its moods, facing it and beating it. And now, in wartime, even that shepherd simile was apt.

Theakston fell silent. Not a man of many words normally, he had talked in spasms, with long gaps. Amory, who knew about Theakston's wife, guessed he had been talking to stop himself thinking. There were times when Amory was glad enough not to have married: the fact that Felicity was dead meant that now he had nothing in the world to worry about. Had she lived, had she married him as had been intended, she would have been his constant worry as well as a brief delight every now and again when he had leave from the sea. He would never have stopped worrying about her; in a sense, like children, wives were hostages to fortune. They could fall ill like the Old Man's wife. Amory was saved all that, now. Or anyway he kidded himself he was: he couldn't forget the bad nights, thinking of what might have been, tossing and turning, flicking on the light over his bunk and smoking one cigarette after another. Or the hours on watch in fair weather and safe water, pacing the bridge with nothing to do but keep an eye on the course and the occasional avoidance of another ship coming up on his starboard bow. That was when a man's thoughts, like the snow in Wensleydale, bit hard. So he could understand Theakston.

'I'll take a look at the chart, Mr Amory.' Captain Theakston came away from the bridge rail and walked into the wheelhouse and then the chartroom. When he came back after a minute he said, 'We're closing the rendezvous position.' He had told Amory, as he was bound to, of the rendezvous but had not gone into any details. 'Half an hour I'd say. Call the Commodore, Mr Amory.'

'Aye, aye, sir.' Amory went to the voice-pipe to Kemp's cabin and blew down it, activating the whistle. Kemp was on the bridge within the minute. After a word with the master he scanned the seas ahead through his binoculars. The light was fading fast now, it would soon be full dark, and the sky was heavily overcast though as yet the snow was still falling only thinly.

'Plenty more up there,' Theakston said.

Kemp nodded. 'Let's hope it holds off for a while.'

'Aye. . . .'

There was no sign of a submarine and no reports had come back from the escort. Fifteen minutes later a blue-shaded lamp started flashing from the Flag: not a contact report, but the expected order to reduce the speed of the convoy. Theakston passed the order down to the engine-room on a nod from Kemp, and the speed of advance came down to seven knots as the ships butted into the sea and the wind and the whirling snowflakes. That snow was already building up on the decks, thin as it was, and the *Hardraw Falls* was mantled in ghostly white, like a shroud, Kemp thought. Sub-Lieutenant Cutler came to the bridge, carrying his own white covering: he had been checking around the guns once again and he looked like an animated snowman.

Kemp caught his eye. 'Almost there, Cutler.' He turned to Theakston. 'What d'you make it now, Captain?'

'Within a mile or two. Mr Amory, have the hands ready with

the jacob's ladder now. Mr Paget to be in charge, with the bosun.' He added, 'Port side amidships.'

Amory passed the word. Below the bridge, shadowy figures moved and there was a clatter as the rolled-up jacob's ladder, rope and wire and wooden treads, was hoisted to the rail ready to be sent down the ship's side along with heavy fenders.

Cutler asked, 'Any contact yet, sir?'

'Not a bloody murmur,' Kemp answered, sounding on edge. He drummed his fingers, half frozen already despite thick gloves, on the teak of the bridge rail. By now they were as near as dammit in position; *Portree* should have picked up the submarine on the Asdics quite a while ago. But there was just nothing. Kemp could not take the *Hardraw Falls* too far beyond the rendezvous. He would in fact very much have liked to do so: if he failed to take off the German agent he would be relieved of a very dirty job.

Now was the time for decision: Theakston reported the ship had reached the rendezvous. Kemp said, 'Very well. No contact. Signalman?'

'Sir?'

'Call up the Flag. Make, "In the absence of contact propose breaking off now in accordance with earlier planning. Request destroyer be detached."'

The signal was flashed across on the blue-shaded Aldis and quickly the reply came back: 'Commodore from Flag, concur. *Portree* will stand by you.'

'Acknowledge,' Kemp said. 'Stop engines, if you please, Captain.'

'I don't like it,' Theakston said.

'No more do I.'

'I have my ship to consider.'

'Yes, I know. I have the convoy to consider. And my orders. The engines will be rung to stop, Captain.'

Theakston shrugged; he had made his protest. He knew the Commodore was under strain; and orders had to be obeyed. He passed the word to Amory and the telegraphs were pulled over. Soon after the engine sounds had ceased and the telegraphs had reported back that the engines were stopped, Theakston ordered the sound signal to indicate that the way was off his ship: the siren gave four short blasts and the ships astern altered to port and starboard to pass along the sides of the *Hardraw Falls*. In the rear of the convoy HMS *Portree* moved up to take station ahead of the Commodore and act as guardship. The other ships moved on, bulky shapes in the darkness – and what had suddenly become a full-scale snowstorm. They were soon lost to sight from the *Hardraw Falls*. And still no contact from beneath the sea.

iv

Below in the engine-room Weller used words similar to Theakston's. 'I don't like it, Chief. Circling like a bloody catherine wheel only not so fast. Too bloody slow in fact.'

'Go fast and you get dizzy.'

'You know what I mean,' Weller said irritably.

'Yes, I know all right. Sitting duck. I'd like to know what's going on. Those buzzes earlier ... something's in the wind, that's for sure.' Sparrow's voice had sounded too loud to be true when the engines had so suddenly been brought to stop and then to slow ahead. 'Maybe this won't last long.'

'Why not ask the bridge, Chief?'

Sparrow laughed. 'You know Theakston. Still, I'll give it a try.' He reached for the voice-pipe, blew down it and put the flexible tube to his ear when the bridge answered.

'Bridge. Captain. What is it?'

'Chief speaking. Wondering what's up, that's all.'

'Nothing to worry about.' Theakston slammed down the cover of the voice-pipe.

'See?' Sparrow said. 'They don't give much away in Yorkshire. Like Scotland, is Yorkshire. Know what they say, do you?' The chief put on what he imagined was a Yorkshire accent. 'Never do owt for nowt, but if thee do, then do it for thissen.'

On the bridge Theakston was thinking that perhaps he could have taken his chief engineer into his confidence. After all, once the German was embarked his presence would be common enough knowledge. But he had been playing safe in informing only Amory : the Commodore was RNR and although he was as basically of the Merchant Service as was Theakston himself, the RN would have rubbed off on him; and you never knew quite

53

where you stood with the King's men. They had a different out-look and at times they could be as thick as a docker's sandwich, though he didn't think Kemp was that.

Theakston said, 'I think we'd do best to increase to nearer half speed, Commodore.'

Kemp nodded. 'I agree. Signalman ... inform *Portree* I'm increasing to seven knots.'

The signal went out: the destroyer was just about visible, keeping station ahead still, circling with the *Hardraw Falls* as the snow came down. Kemp cursed to himself: the blizzard was making life extremely difficult at just about the worst possible time. It was as he was thinking this that the destroyer's Aldis started flashing again.

'Contact, sir,' Corrigan reported. 'Bearing red four five, an echo, distant one mile and closing.'

A U-boat, or the British submarine?

Almost certainly it must be the latter, though coincidences could occur. Kemp was taking no chances. Action stations had in fact been sounded at the time the *Hardraw Falls* had detached from the convoy, just so that all hands were on the top line and ready. Now Kemp sent Cutler down to warn the guns' crews aft; and at the same time Theakston used the voice-pipe to the engine-room and warned Sparrow that there might be an attack. From then on the men were on a knife-edge above and below as they waited for the unknown, the unpredictable. It became a time for breath holding, for wonderment, on the part of the ma-jority not in the know, that the destroyer wasn't attacking: there was no reverberation from depth-charges going off. Kemp felt a shake in his hands as he peered uselessly through the snow-filled darkness. If he had miscalculated, a torpedo might strike at any moment.

SIX

In the submarine's main control room the lieutenant in command stood by the housed periscope, with von Hagen under guard and ready to be taken up to the conning-tower as soon as the boat surfaced for the transfer. All was quiet, little sound beyond the hum of the motors and clicks from the gyro repeater as the coxswain moved the wheel from time to time. There was a curious feeling in the boat: no one cared much for having a Nazi agent aboard and there would be a strong sense of relief when he'd been disembarked.

The air would be cleaner: there was dirt sticking in large quantities to any Jerry spy and word had gone through the boat that this one was particularly unclean in what he'd been up to in Norway. Not that he looked the sort of bastard the galley wireless said he was. He had a strong face but not a sadistic one; indeed he looked like anyone's father, missed back home and anxious himself to get back to the wife and kids. Tall and thin with a haunted look in his face as if his world had come to an end, which of course it had. Get the sod back to the UK, and after the interrogation he might swing. Or they might keep him till the war was over and then hang him. None of the submarine's ratings knew quite what the law in wartime said about captured spies but there was a general belief that they could be hanged, unless that applied only to traitors, British subjects caught out in passing information to the enemy. Whatever his future might be, the Jerry had been made aware since the pick-up that he wasn't welcome. Loud comments and a fist now and again as the sod had been led from one part of the boat to another, to be taken to the heads and such. Not when an officer was present, because the orders had been very clear, but the officers couldn't be everywhere at once.

The submarine moved ahead for the rendezvous position; a little late. There had been some trouble with the diesels, causing delay, but now they were not far off. The lieutenant in command said as much to von Hagen.

The German smiled. 'You'll be glad to be rid of me.'

'Oh, you've been no trouble.' This was true: von Hagen had been a model prisoner; and well enough aware of his unpopularity not to be arrogant, not to mention the name of his Führer or refer in any way to the Third Reich. He might have been an Englishman: he spoke the language perfectly and had good manners, the manners of an English gentleman. In other circumstances he might have been a good friend: the lieutenant was almost sorry for him, facing at best captivity in the UK ... it had occurred to the lieutenant to wonder why von Hagen was being put aboard a ship bound for Russia but he'd put the thought behind him. It wasn't his concern. Just a matter of convenience, probably: the outward bound PQ was passing at the right moment, whereas the next homeward convoy out of Russia would have meant too much hanging about.

'Coming up to the position, sir,' the navigator reported. 'Three miles, dead ahead as she goes.'

'Right. Stand by to surface.' As the boat moved ahead and the order was given to blow main tanks the lieutenant took up his position at the periscope, stood back as the great steel shaft surged up from its stowage ready to break through the sea into the wind and snow. He glanced briefly at the German's face: it had a tight, defeated look, even a sadness.

ii

'Submarine on the surface, sir, red eight five – '

'Can you identify?'

'She's making the identification signal now, sir.'

'Thank God,' Kemp said, blowing out his cheeks. 'Make the answer, Corrigan.' He put a hand on Theakston's shoulder. 'I'd like the ladder down now, Captain. And the ship stopped for the transfer.' He watched the bearing through his binoculars, dreading the moment he met von Hagen, or more precisely the moment when he had to follow his orders and put an old friend under threat and worse. The boat was only just visible as she made her approach, visible only from the white curfuffle at her stern, just a blur in the foul weather conditions. But within the next couple of minutes she was lying close off the merchant ship's port side, nosing in to bring the fore casing up to the lowered fenders below the dangling jacob's ladder. From the bridge Kemp saw the figures in the conning-tower, saw the fore hatch open and a man emerge followed by two others. The central one was obviously von Hagen, with a rifle at his back, a bayoneted rifle. Snow swirled with the wind, at times obscuring the submarine, but through it Kemp saw the German being propelled along the casing towards the jacob's ladder, saw the rating in the lead reach out to grab for the line dangling from the foot of the ladder and haul it close. As he did so, a seaman aboard the *Hardraw Falls* sent a line snaking down to be caught by a man on the submarine's casing and attached around the waist of the prisoner. When this had been done Kemp heard the shouted, rough command: 'All right now. *Up* you go!'

The German stepped to the jacob's ladder, unaccompanied but with the rifle aimed. The line was hauled taut as he climbed, tended by the man from the deck above: a prisoner could drop in the drink if he preferred the quick end in an icy sea. Alongside Kemp, Theakston commented on the precaution. 'I dare say you'd rather he went,' he said.

Kemp gave a harsh laugh. 'The answer to that is yes. But I suppose it's cowardly of me to want that. Isn't it?'

'I'd not say so, no. There'll be worse facing him in Russian hands.'

Kemp thought: don't, for God's sake, rub it in! But Theakston had meant well. As von Hagen reached the deck, hands took him and helped him to find his feet. Leaning over the bridge rail, Kemp called down to the submarine CO, 'Thank you, Captain, and well done.'

'Nothing in it, sir.'

'So you say! Off with you now – and a safe journey home.' Kemp waved a hand, the lieutenant saluted and passed the orders to take the submarine off the side of the *Hardraw Falls*. The boat was soon lost in the snow and the night; Kemp imagined she would probably submerge. The conditions would be a damn sight easier inside the hull than keeping a watch in the conning-tower. He said, 'Well, there we are, Captain. Now let's press on and rejoin the convoy.'

Theakston went into the wheelhouse and passed the order down to the engine-room for full ahead. On the starting platform Sparrow gave a sigh of relief as the shafts began spinning and he felt the screws grip the water. Theakston had said the Commodore wanted the maximum possible speed in order to overtake the convoy. Sparrow was going to give him all he wanted: it wasn't a happy feeling, to be on their own apart from just the one destroyer.

On the bridge Cutler asked, 'Do you want to see the German now, sir?'

'No,' Kemp said. 'I'm remaining on the bridge and I don't want him up here. I'll see him when I go down, Cutler.'

'Very good, sir.'

'As for you – go and get your head down.'

'I'm all right, sir, thank you.'

'Do as you're told, Cutler. I don't want an assistant half doped for lack of sleep.'

iii

'A bloody Jerry,' Petty Officer Napper said in a surly tone, 'and it seems he's being given a *cabin*! What's the idea, might I ask?'

'Commodore's orders is all I know, same as you,' Chief Steward Buckle said. 'Don't agree with 'em myself, but there you are, eh? Treat the bugger proper, the Commodore said. Allocate him a steward, the Old Man followed up with. My arse! He'll have to share Torrence with the Old Man and Kemp and they can make the best they can of it. I suppose he'll be guarded?'

'He will and all. My guns' crews depleted, three 'ands working in watches on the bugger's door.'

'Armed, of course?'

'Of course.'

Buckle scratched his head reflectively. 'Well, that's something. Take over the ship else, he could!'

'Stretch of imagination. What d'you think my lads'd be doing, to let that 'appen?' Napper walked away, conscious that he was coming into his own: PO of the Guard – on a wanted spy! A bloody, stinking Hun with the rank of Colonel so he'd been told. One of Hitler's thugs. Or maybe not quite that: he wasn't Gestapo, anyway not one of the ordinary ones. More like an infiltrator into the Resistance and doubtless responsible for a good many deaths and tortures. The way he'd been put aboard, he must be someone of importance ... Napper preened himself. The Nazi would be good for a number of free drinks in Napper's local when he got back home, so long as he was allowed to talk about it, that was, and most likely in fact he wouldn't. The brass was hot on secrecy and Napper might have to wait for glory till after the war was over. So far he didn't even know the Jerry's name. No one did, except the nobs on the bridge presumably. And it rankled with Napper that according to Mr Cutler the Jerry was to be addressed as 'sir'. Sir, to a Nazi!

'You,' Napper said, emerging up the ladder on to the after superstructure. 'You, Able Seaman Grove.'

'Me, PO?'

'That's what I just said, isn't it? Now, Watch and Quarter Bill. Right?'

'Watch and *what*?'

'You 'eard. Posting of the guard on the Nazi.' Napper felt snappish: perhaps Watch and Quarter Bill was a somewhat grandiose way of referring to the posting of a sentry, but still, Grove had sounded a shade too supercilious. 'You'll take the morning watch on 'is cabin, relieve whatsisname – Park. All right?'

'Yes, PO.'

'An' after that, we'll see.' It was an intricate business, working out watchkeeping rotas, and it took time and thought. You couldn't denude the guns just for a Jerry but on the other hand you couldn't denude an important Nazi agent just for guns, which were pretty useless anyway, decoration mostly, bloody ornaments, though Napper would never have thus denigrated his job this time yesterday, before he'd become gaoler to a high-powered Hun. Napper, as he went down the ladder, was conscious of Grove's long stare behind his back, but he didn't know what Grove was thinking. Later, when he took over guard duty, Grove released his thoughts to Ordinary Seaman Park.

'That Napper.' He told Park about the PO's reference to the Watch and Quarter Bill. 'Anyone'd think he was chief gunner's mate aboard the bloody *Nelson* or such ... working out the watches for fifteen 'undred matloes – port and starboard, red, white and blue, first and second parts thereof, blimey! Action stations, collision stations, fire stations, duties part of ship, duty 'ands of the watch, who falls in when Both Watches is piped, ditto when Both Watches of the *'Ands* is piped. So on and so forth. And God knows how the daft bugger ever made leading 'and, let alone PO.' Grove sniffed. 'He'd make heavy weather of being bosun's mate of a dinghy, would our Napper!'

Having taken over guard duties, Grove bent and peered, or tried to peer, through the slats of the jalousied door. By order of Kemp, the light was to remain on. Grove didn't get much of a view but he reckoned the Nazi was on his bunk and probably sleeping.

iv

When the dawn came up, slowly and with difficulty, to reveal an iron-grey, overcast sky and a restless, leaden sea, the *Hardraw Falls* was snow-covered virtually everywhere from truck to main deck. There were black patches around the funnel casing and the funnel itself stood out and that was all except for the guns, kept clear by the hands on watch. It was a ship in outline only : no visible hatch covers, no anchor cables and no slips or clenches on the fo'c'sle. Even the ladders had their treads under the mantle of white. There was a thick layer on monkey's island, and along the bridge wings Kemp's footsteps led in pits three or four inches deep.

And it was snowing still.

So far no convoy : that was not surprising, though a landsman might think it so when only some thirty-five sea miles had been lost whilst waiting about for the submarine. A ship with only about a knot of speed in hand over and above the speed of the convoy might well take around thirty hours to catch up the tail end. Theakston, who had remained on the bridge all night with Kemp, yawned and rubbed hard at eyes that stung with lack of sleep. His face was blue with the cold: he brushed snow from it with an automaton-like movement of a gloved hand. Blast the war, he thought: in peacetime he had never come this far north. Britain's trade had never been with the Soviets. And now half his mind was in Whitby: so long since he'd had word about Dora. Alive still – or not? But no use thinking, worrying; he must concentrate on the bitter sea, on its potential for danger, on moving towards Russia. He said, zombie-like as Kemp came to rest at his side, 'I reckon we just plug on. . . .'

'H'm?'

'The convoy. Catching up.'

'That's about it.' Kemp peered through the murk, through the whirling snow. He was as cold as charity but, although daylight had come, he was reluctant to go below. A ship's bridge was familiar ground; in every sense of the phrase he knew exactly where he stood. When he went below he would step into an un-familiar world the moment he confronted von Hagen: a web of broken promises, of bare-faced lies, of deceiving a man who would look upon him as a friend at court, a man he had sailed with so many times. Thus he lingered, postponing what he was under orders to do, and was there when Cutler came up.

'Breakfast, sir.'

'You've had yours?'

'Sure I did, sir.' Cutler hesitated. 'The prisoner . . . he's talked to the sentry. He's asking to see you. Asking by name, sir: Cap-tain Kemp, he said.'

Kemp nodded: so von Hagen knew, or anyway had been struck by the name, which he could have heard one of the ship's crew or the naval party mentioning. The German wouldn't have been able to identify anyone on the bridge in the darkness of the embarkation from the submarine but if he'd picked up the name he would want to know if the Kemp aboard the *Hardraw Falls* and the Captain Kemp he'd known were one and the same. Kemp said, 'All right, Cutler. I'll go down to my cabin. Give me half an hour, then have the prisoner brought in. The escort to remain outside my door.'

In his cabin Kemp washed and shaved and then his steward

brought in his breakfast. He ate without appetite, making short work of it, wanting only to get to the coffee and cigarette stage. Precisely half an hour after he had left the bridge, the knock came at his door: Cutler.

'Prisoner present, sir.'

'Thank you, Cutler. Bring him in.' Kemp had stiffened as if expecting a physical blow. He lit another cigarette, with shaking fingers that he couldn't hold still. From the door Cutler jerked his head, saying nothing. Von Hagen came in alone. Cutler said, 'I'll be outside, sir.' Cutler had tact. The door closed behind him.

Von Hagen's eyes had widened with pleasure. 'So it *is* you, Captain Kemp.'

'Yes. A long time. . . .' Kemp held out his hand; the German took it in a strong grip. 'The war brings changes, von Hagen. I'm sorry.'

'So am I. They were pleasant days, the days of peaceful sailing.'

'Yes.' Kemp gestured to a chair and offered his cigarette case and a lighter. The German drew in smoke thankfully as he sat down.

'You asked to see me, von Hagen.'

'To meet an old friend, if you were the same Kemp. That was all. Not to ask favours. I accept that we are enemies now.' The German's look was direct, no shifting away from Kemp's eyes. 'I've lost – that's all.' He paused. 'Have the years, the years of war, treated you well, Captain?'

Kemp shrugged. 'Well enough – I'm still alive and that's something.'

'But not still with the Mediterranean-Australia Line. A Commodore of your naval reserve, I see. You are not captain of the ship?'

Kemp said, 'I'm the Commodore of the convoy, von Hagen.'

'I was not told – I was told nothing. And you are returning from Russia, from Murmansk or Archangel – or should I not ask?' Von Hagen gave a quiet laugh. 'I am, after all, an enemy –'

'Yes. But you may ask . . . and I shall answer.' Kemp found the words coming with difficulty, almost as though he had developed a speech defect. 'The convoy is not returning from Russia, Colonel von Hagen. It is out of Iceland . . . bound for Archangel.'

The German's face had reacted: there was total surprise, almost shock. 'That will be dangerous for me, Commodore. The Russians . . . however, I am, of course, a British prisoner of war. But suppose the ship is searched, what then? British prisoner or not – '

Kemp said steadily, 'The ship will not be searched, that I can guarantee. The Russians are our allies, not our masters, and no search will be permitted.'

Von Hagen relaxed and blew out his breath. 'I'm relieved! The Russians and I don't mix. If I were to be found, well, it would be the end after interrogation by – '

'I realize that – '

'But in British hands . . . it's not to be welcomed, I need hardly say, but at least I know your people behave properly. As I said, Commodore – I've lost, and that's the way it goes.'

'Yes. You're philosophical, von Hagen – very.'

The German smiled. 'I have no option, and I always look on the bright side. I always did, if you remember.'

'I remember.' Kemp did: sometimes von Hagen's business trips had not been as successful as he'd hoped, but he'd never been disturbed. There was always another day, he used to say, always another chance. The same with women: von Hagen had had an eye for them, and he was an attractive man, but sometimes he'd made a wrong choice and ended up with the equivalent – or once the reality – of a slapped face, but that too he had always shrugged off and had come up smiling. He hadn't much to smile about now but was taking it well – because he was bound for British hands, not Russian. No doubt there had always been the possibility of being taken by the Russians; at least he'd been spared that – or so he believed.

Kemp licked at dry lips, searching for the right words, the best way of shattering an illusion. Before he had formulated what he was going to say there was an interruption. His voice-pipe whined and he answered. 'Commodore – '

'Bridge, sir, chief officer speaking. Weather's clearing – '

'Any sign of the convoy?'

'No, sir, but the masthead lookout reports wreckage ahead, fine on the port bow, looks like woodwork in a big patch of oil.'

Kemp said, 'I'll be up, Amory. Better inform *Portree*.' He

turned to von Hagen. 'We'll talk again later, Colonel.' He called for Cutler, and the German was taken back to his cabin under escort. Kemp felt as though he had been reprieved.

SEVEN

Theakston had reached the bridge and all the binoculars were on the wreckage. It was heaving up and down, sliding over the swell, disappearing now and again. There was no snow now and the visibility was fair to good, the sky clearing fast. The cold was worse than ever and each breath was like a knife-thrust in the lungs.

'One of the convoy?' Theakston asked.

'I fear so.'

'You'd think there'd be more.'

'Could be a single straggler, the usual arse-end Charlie,' Kemp said. Arse-end Charlies – like themselves currently – were always at extra risk. You couldn't stop or even slow for just one ship, and you only detached a warship to stand guard if you had a big enough escort, which was not the case this time – the *Hardraw Falls* herself wouldn't have been given a destroyer if it hadn't been for the importance of embarking von Hagen and delivering him to Russia safely.

Three minutes after Kemp had reached the bridge there was another report from the masthead: a boat, some distance beyond the wreckage, a ship's lifeboat and a man waving from it. Theakston didn't wait for orders: he told Amory to alter towards the boat and have men standing by the jacob's ladder.

Kemp demurred. He said, 'We'll leave them to the destroyer, Captain. There's a doctor aboard. Corrigan?'

'Yessir?'

'Ask *Portree* to pick up survivors.'

'Aye, aye, sir.'

'And add that I wish to be informed immediately of any news

of the convoy.' Kemp watched anxiously as the destroyer swept up towards the wreckage. As she slowed her engines the lifeboat was lost to view behind her hull; but within a short time she was once again moving fast and heeling under full port helm to circle back towards the *Hardraw Falls*. As she came up on the Commodore's port beam her loud hailer came on.

There was an amplified shout across the water: 'Commodore ahoy!'

Kemp waved an arm from the bridge wing, and took the megaphone handed him by Cutler. He called back in response. 'How many and where from?'

'Six men in the boat, only two alive, sir. From a freighter, ss *City of Khartoum*. Convoy came under U-boat attack. Two ships known to be lost ... could be more.' There was a pause. 'One U-boat sunk, sir. Our survivors don't know how many there were.'

'We could be steaming right into it.'

'Yes, sir. Any orders?'

'No change,' Kemp said. 'We press on to rejoin the convoy. I take it they're holding their course?'

They were, *Portree*'s captain said. Kemp waved a hand again and turned away. The *Hardraw Falls* would join the battle, if it was still going on when they caught up, with her armament useless against U-boats unless and until one of them was forced to the surface by depth-charge attack from the A/S screen and the destroyers.

Kemp remarked on this to Cutler.

Cutler said, 'You have a dilemma, sir.'

'Have I?' Kemp raised his eyebrows. 'I didn't know I had.'

'Well ... maybe you don't, sir. But it occurred to me ... that is ... we're putting another ship, us, at risk unnecessarily. We have a valuable cargo. And like you've just said, we don't add anything to the fire power.'

'Just a target.'

'In a nutshell, sir – yes.'

'We could just bugger off?'

'Well now, I guess – '

Kemp said evenly, 'It did go through my mind, Cutler, and it went right out again. Of course, you're quite right to bring it up.

66

But there are two points that come uppermost. The first is that I'm the Commodore. It's my convoy. I have a duty to be there, Cutler.'

'Yes, sir. And the second?'

Kemp gave a mirthless grin. 'It's a hundred to one we'll meet the U-boats in any event, returning to base.'

Cutler nodded. He had half a mind to tell the Commodore that he could deviate, alter course westwards and get the hell out until the returning U-boats had made it south past their position, but he didn't say this. He could guess what Kemp's answer would be, and as for him, he hadn't come over to avoid action. Once again he recalled the words of the RCNVR's theme song: *We came over for the fighting, not the fun. . . .*

That conversation reached the crew of the *Hardraw Falls* via the agency of the seaman on lookout in the port wing of the bridge.

ii

'He's got no right,' Chief Steward Buckle said. 'What bloody use are we anyway, I ask you!'

Buckle had encountered the bosun, who had been checking the fire hydrants along with the second engineer: orders from the bridge, since they might be in need of the fire hoses any time now. Jock Tawney said indifferently, 'I don't reckon that's the point.'

'Oh. What is, then?'

'We're the Commodore's ship, that's what. The Commodore don't scarper from trouble.'

'I don't see why not, Bose.'

'P'raps you don't.' Tawney sniffed; in his view chief stewards thought only of lining their own pockets, which was why they'd gone to sea in the first place, and Buckle saw no profit in this, only danger. The danger was there, all right; but it was always there at sea in wartime, just part of the job and you got on with it. Meanwhile Buckle was getting on with his complaint.

He said, 'The Russians stand to lose a lot of bloody ammo. They won't like that.'

'Let 'em shove it, then.'

'Christ Almighty, Bose, they're the whole reason we're here!'

67

'More's the pity,' Tawney said, and turned his back. Buckle shrugged; no point in saying any more. Like all seamen, Tawney was thick as a plank. Horny-handed shellbacks, haulers on ropes and tackles, no intelligence but thought they were bloody marvellous just because they *were* seamen . . . Buckle carried on along the alleyway to his cabin, where he had some stores lists to go through. The ship was short on a few provisions, items that couldn't be obtained in enough quantity in UK ports: the war was nothing but shortages. Most likely the Russians would be unable to top up but he would try. Buckle toyed with thoughts of caviar. That should be plentiful, with luck. Probably not much would be eaten aboard and if he could buy in quantity there might be something in it for himself when they got back to home waters, a really good profit from under the noses of the company. If they didn't go and get bloody sunk in the meantime.

Bugger Kemp!

And bugger that Jerry too, Buckle thought. If the brass in Berlin happened to have got word that he'd been nabbed and put aboard the *Hardraw Falls*, well then, obviously they'd be trying especially hard to knock the ship off before he got where he was going and was made to spill a whole lot of beans. . . .

Beans . . . Heinz. Chief Steward Buckle's mind clicked smoothly on to matters within his province. Baked beans were a vital part of the crew's menu and were one of the items he was short of. He didn't know if Russians ate baked beans.

iii

'You there, Corrigan.'

Corrigan looked up: he was sitting at the naval mess table, writing a letter home for posting in Archangel, knowing it would get to his parents no quicker than if he posted it in a UK port on return but wanting to get it off just in case he didn't make it on the homeward run. 'Yes, PO?'

'Letter writing!' Napper clicked his tongue. 'Action alarm might go any time.'

'That's right. Commodore didn't want to have the hands closed up before it was necessary, so –'

'I know that, thank you. Soft-'earted, is Kemp. And bloody right to press on,' Napper said rather surprisingly. He wasn't usually all that keen, Corrigan thought. But now he was leading up to something and it began to emerge. 'Said you was a makee-learn doctor, right? I need an opinion.'

Corrigan nodded, sighed and pushed his writing pad aside. Perhaps it was good practice for after the war. 'What seems to be the trouble?' he asked.

'Dunno. That's for you to say ... I mean, if you'd do me a favour, that is.'

'Of course I will, short of opening you up, PO.'

Napper blenched. 'I never bloody asked – '

'I know, I know. Just my way of saying I'm not on the medical register and it's little I can advise in fact. I'm not supposed to pronounce at all, actually.'

Actually. No doubt about it, Corrigan was officer material. Napper said, 'Exigencies o' war ... exentuating circumstances.'

'All right, PO. Let's have it.'

'I gets a funny feeling,' Napper said, screwing up his face in undiagnosed discomfort.

'Where?'

'All over like.'

'When?'

'When? Never know when it's coming on, do I?'

'When there's a U-boat contact?'

Napper glared. 'None o' your lip, Corrigan. I didn't ask for cheek. And the answer's no ... not specially then.'

'I see. I think you said the doctor aboard *Nottingham* prescribed Black Draught?'

'Yes! 'E did an' all!'

'Very effective stuff, PO.'

'Well, 'e can stuff it, effective or not.'

Corrigan grinned. 'Talking of stuffing it ... there was a well worn joke that used to make the rounds of the medical schools and probably still does. A chap went to his doctor, said he was suffering from constipation ... the doctor prescribed suppositories. A fortnight later, the chap went back and said he'd taken them twice daily as instructed but for all the good they'd done, he might just as well have shoved them up his arse.' He paused; Napper's face was blank. 'You don't get it?'

69

'Don't sound too likely. To swallow suppositories, they're bloody poisonous, aren't they?'

Corrigan said, 'I expect so, yes, but never mind, it was just a joke.'

'I don't reckon doctors ought to make jokes like that. I'm being serious. There's something wrong. Maybe it's me nerves. Think it could be?'

'I simply don't know. I hadn't got very far in medicine, hadn't even taken my anatomy exams.'

'Taken?'

'Yes, but they're not suppositories, PO.'

iv

The shout came from the masthead lookout: 'Torpedo trail starboard, sir . . . green four five!'

Kemp brought his binoculars up; Cutler beat him to it. 'Got it, sir. Two of them.' He pointed. 'There.'

'Right.' The twin trails, some two cables'-lengths apart, had now come up clear in Kemp's lenses. He called out, 'Steer between them, Captain! Starboard your helm.'

Theakston gave the order: in the wheelhouse the helm went over. Theakston sounded the alarm and Kemp watched closely as the ship's head came round to starboard. The master checked the swing as the bows came to a point midway between the torpedo trails.

'Port ten . . . midships . . . *steady*!'

In the wheelhouse the helmsman met the swing and steadied his course on 046 degrees, saw the thin marks just beneath the surface as they raced towards the ship. Kemp was holding his breath now, staring ahead, staring down the starboard side as the torpedoes closed. One of them passed no more than a dozen yards clear. From the port side, Cutler called out that the second torpedo had also passed: Theakston's judgment had been spot on, but the attack was only just starting, unless the U-boat had no more fish left, the others expended on the convoy ahead, between the *Hardraw Falls* and the North Cape. Kemp found his fists clenched tight: the ship was a bloody great target. The Nazis couldn't miss a second time. But by now *Portree* was flying the attack signal and moving in at high speed, following the

70

pings of her Asdic, water flinging back from her fo'c'sle and the depth-charge racks and throwers ready aft. Aboard the Commodore's ship the close-range weapons were manned in the bridge wings, on monkey's island, and on the after superstructure. Kemp looked around: if only the U-boat could be forced to the surface ... it was time that his gunnery rates were given a chance to show what they could do.

Kemp saw Petty Officer Napper moving along the after welldeck, coming for'ard, an anxious expression on his long, gloomy face. This, unknown to Kemp, was due to the action alarm having cut short Napper's medical consultation. Corrigan had been in the process of giving him some good advice, having got his rotten jokes out of the way, and Hitler had buggered it all up. Corrigan had suggested *inter alia* that Napper should go and see the doctor again, and when Napper had retorted that the quack was about as useful as a whore at a wedding, Corrigan had said he could do worse than put in a request to see a Russian doctor in Archangel. At first Napper had refused absolutely to see a Russian quack, a bloody Communist, but Corrigan, who had had enough of Napper though he didn't let it show, had gone on about the Russians having a lot of advanced knowledge and medical technology and more resources ashore than any ship could have. Napper had been much impressed: Leading Signalman Corrigan was nearly half a doctor, and doctors were important people even if some of them didn't know much, and then there was that very special way in which Corrigan said the word 'actually'. A proper gent, was Corrigan.

Napper's expression of anxiety as he hurried about his gun positions was due to a snag: in order to see a Russian quack, he would have to tell the surgeon commander aboard the *Nottingham*, if ever they made Archangel, that he was too bloody useless to be consulted again. That would take some doing. In the meantime, Napper's stomach was playing him up. He saw a connection with his chest: after all, the two parts were adjacent.

Proceeding for'ard, Napper reached the ladder leading to the midship superstructure just as the *Portree*'s first pattern of depth-charges went up. Napper took the steps fast and arrived on monkey's island panting. Away to starboard the sea was heaving up, boiling water breaking surface in great humps, but no U-boat. Napper checked around the guns.

71

'All right, lads?'

'Yes, PO.'

'Give the buggers hell if they surface,' Napper said, sounding efficient. Then he saw Sub-Lieutenant Cutler coming up the ladder from the bridge.

'Hey there, Napper. Petty Officer Napper.'

'Yessir?'

Cutler reached out and tapped Napper's arm. 'Not so warlike, okay? Remember the orders – no firing except on the order from the bridge, all right?'

'Yes,' Napper said, scowling. Little git. Little *Yankee* git! It was no wonder he didn't feel well. Cutler was enough to give the cat kittens. Cowboys from Texas just didn't fit the sea scene, they were born and bred to be soldiers.

v

There were no more torpedoes: the U-boat was apparently operating singly and there was no way of knowing whether or not it had been part of the attack on the main PQ convoy. But the gunners were going to get their chance even if it wasn't much: *Portree*'s attack, one pattern after another going down with different depth settings on the charges, was effective. The reverberations shattered through the plating of the *Hardraw Falls*, ringing like deep-toned bells in the engine-room and boiler-room, shaking Buckle's office where he was obeying company's orders by gathering up invoices and requisitions and other ship's papers and stuffing them into the big safe with all the cash – aboard the Bricker Dockett ships the chief steward acted also as purser – so that they would go to the bottom rather than float to the possible benefit of the enemy, though Buckle often wondered, why the hell bother? It wouldn't help Hitler much to be in possession of corned beef bills, though possibly it would give away the identity of the supply ports which he might then decide to bomb, but since he bombed them anyway it didn't really seem important.

The job done, Buckle slammed the safe door shut and twirled the combination locks which he'd set to the date of his former mother-in-law's birthday, making the old bag a damn sight more important than she'd ever imagined. Then he went up on deck, circumspectly. Basically anyone was safer on deck than down below, but Buckle didn't want to stop a personal bullet or shell if the U-boat surfaced and attacked by gunfire.

But he wasn't due for that, not yet.

He heard a rising shout along the decks, a shout – almost a baying – of triumph, a real blood-lust, Buckle thought. Not far ahead, a little to starboard of the ship's track, he saw the long, low, black shape, the conning-tower manned by a press of Nazis, officers and ratings, some of whom were spilling over on to the fore casing and running for the gun platform for'ard of the conning-tower. The boat had a list on her as though she'd taken something that had caused some plates to be sprung, and there was smoke drifting up from the conning-tower. But she wasn't done yet and the gun was coming to bear. That U-boat, Buckle thought, she's bloody close, and getting closer.

vi

The U-boat had been forced to the surface fine on the starboard bow of the *Hardraw Falls* and distant little more than six cables – not quite as close in fact as Buckle had estimated. Kemp had brought the guns' crews to readiness to open. Theakston asked, 'Do you want to turn away, Commodore?'

'No point. I'm going to close – and pray! Take her in, please, Captain.'

'You don't mean ram the bugger?'

'I do. A course to ram, as close to the conning-tower as you can make it.'

'But my bows! They may not take the impact.'

'We must chance it. It's our only hope if – ' Kemp broke off, ducking instinctively as he saw the flash from the U-boat. *Portree* was racing in now but seemed unable to bear with her guns since she had the *Hardraw Falls* immediately behind the target. Theakston was forging on now, heading for the U-boat: the two vessels were close. The first shell from the Nazi went over the bridge, the second took the foremast and carried it away in a tangle of wire and shattered wood, some of it falling across the port wing of the bridge and only just missing Cutler. The masthead lookout was thrown clear, coming down in the water off the ship's port beam. Then the *Hardraw Falls* hit, a glancing blow but a heavy one, immediately below the conning-tower, a crunch that sent the U-boat heeling over to starboard, flinging men into the water. The ship gave a lurch as the speed came off suddenly. Everywhere men went sprawling: Petty Officer Napper spun along the after well-deck, legs and arms flying, to fetch up in the scuppers and half-way through a washport: he was jammed there helpless and swearing as, on the order from the bridge, the close-range weapons opened on the Nazis. Chief Steward Buckle was flung back against a bulkhead, only partially cushioned by a sizeable rump. Kemp found himself pressed against the fore rail of the bridge, just for a moment. He looked across at the U-boat: he could see she wasn't going to last – the blow from the *Hardraw Falls* had completed the work begun by the *Portree*'s depth-charge attack. The close-range weapons were proving deadly: the casing was strewn with bodies, some of which had slid into the sea, trailing blood.

'She's going, sir,' Cutler said. The list had increased suddenly.

'Yes. Cease firing, Cutler.'

Cutler passed the word. The order was not immediately obeyed: the crews of the after guns had the bit between their teeth now. The Nazis were in their sights and were going to get it, right up to the end. Cutler took up the Commodore's megaphone and yelled through it.

'Bloody cease firing! Obey the order!' His voice got through and there was quiet as the rattle of the guns stopped.

'Where's Napper, for Jeez' sake?'

A voice came back: 'Jammed, sir.'

'Unjam him, then!'

vii

There was no damage to the bow: Amory had checked round. There had been no chance to retrieve the masthead lookout before the cold killed him. The U-boat had gone down, taking most of her dead with her. Kemp left the bridge feeling dead tired and somewhat sick: the slaughter had been very bloody and there could be no excuse for disobedience of orders, for the continued shooting-up of a defeated enemy who had lost the means to hit back. On the other hand, Kemp could understand only too well the blood-lust that had taken over. In the sea war you didn't often get to close grips with the enemy, you didn't often see the whites of their eyes as it were, but you suffered from them just the same. You suffered via your families, your home under threat from the Luftwaffe, via sons or brothers or fathers who perhaps had bought it in other actions on land or sea or in the air, you suffered via the everlasting days and weeks and months of wondering when you were going to be knocked off by a U-boat or in air or surface attack. When you got the enemy in your gunsights, then you reacted. It was only natural. Even so, disobedience of orders couldn't ever be allowed to go by default. Kemp had some bollocking to do. But there was something else first: von Hagen. That interrupted conversation – Kemp now wanted to get the matter off his chest as soon as possible, though he knew it couldn't be settled in five minutes. There might have to be many sessions, and he must have his mind in order before arrival in Archangel. He told off Cutler to bring the German to his cabin again, and once again to wait outside with the armed escort.

Von Hagen came in. He said, 'One to you, I'm told.'

'Yes. And I'm not gloating, von Hagen.'

'You're not the sort to do that, I know.'

Kemp stared at him as he sat down. 'And you?'

Von Hagen shrugged. 'I doubt if I would gloat but I can't really say. My war hasn't been in the field . . . not the battlefield, I mean.'

'But in Norway?'

'I don't believe I follow. . . .'

'The Resistance. When you broke the enclaves, as probably you did from time to time . . . and caused men's deaths. Women's too, perhaps. What were your feelings then, von Hagen?'

'I tried not to have them. I did my duty.'

'And hardened your heart.' Kemp pushed himself back in his chair. 'Yes, I understand. Or I think I do.'

Von Hagen shook his head. 'I think this, Captain – it is different for you, for all the British people – '

'In what way?'

Once again von Hagen shrugged. 'Britain is a democracy, with a kindly, gentlemanly King. You are fighters, yes, but you are not fanatics for any cause, like us Germans – '

'I didn't think – before the war – that you were a fanatical Nazi, von Hagen.'

'No. I don't think I am now either. But I am very anti-communist.'

'Yes, I knew that. That's your fanaticism?'

'Yes. A fanaticism in an "anti" sense.'

Kemp got to his feet and went over to the square port, looking out over the bows thrusting into the cold sea. He kept his back turned to the German as he asked, 'Tell me this: what are your views on Hitler?'

'I think that is an unfair question.' There was a rebuke in von Hagen's tone. 'Herr Hitler is my Führer, my Chancellor. It would be unbecoming in me to criticize.'

'Yet I still ask the question.' Kemp swung round and met von Hagen's eyes. 'And I believe – reading between the lines of what you've just said – that in fact you have got criticisms.'

'Have you no criticisms of Mr Churchill?'

'Sometimes, yes. In Britain, we're free to have them. But of course there's no lack of trust, no lack of belief that in basis Churchill's conducting the war properly.'

'And you suggest – am I right – that we in Germany haven't the same belief in Herr Hitler?'

'Yes,' Kemp said. He said it with a touch of defiance. He was out of his depth and he knew it, knew he wasn't putting anything across effectively. What he wanted to say was that trust in Hitler was surely impossible, that no normal person could believe, for instance, that persecution of whole sections of the German community was a good thing, that a leader who was reliably said to act upon his intuition rather than upon considered advice was anything better than a charlatan ... that, and a lot more. The atrocities in the occupied countries, of which von Hagen must know plenty; the waging of the war at sea against women and children – the sinking, early in hostilities, of the *Athenia* crossing the Atlantic with all those children aboard; so very many things that had left a blot on civilization to the horror of intelligent men and women.

Kemp didn't say any of that: he must not antagonize von Hagen too far. But he very much wanted to know the German's thoughts because he needed to make a fresh assessment of an old friend who had been changed by war. If he could perhaps begin to make von Hagen see things differently, get him to question the validity of his loyalty to a mass murderer who was far from sane, if he could get inside the man's mind – then he might probe out something useful, in accordance with his orders but without the need to utter distasteful threats.

It was going to be an uphill task for any convoy Commodore, a plain seaman without political frills.

viii

One of those who was particularly disturbed by the fact of having a Nazi aboard was an able seaman of the ship's crew – Able Seaman Swile, a cockney with a mean face, a closed face with a slit for a mouth. That meanness could have been with him from birth or it could have become superimposed by the events in Swile's life, which had not been an easy one. The family background was not good: his father, who had died when Swile had been two years of age, had been replaced by a stepfather who had detested him and had gone to prison for beating him black and blue and breaking an arm and a leg on different occasions. Swile had mostly played truant from school, had left as soon as he could and drifted into crime of a petty nature – and had begun flirting with the Communist Party. Swile had been in his late teens at the time Mosley's British Union of Fascists had been at their zenith and he'd had many brushes with them. More than brushes: he'd been beaten up more effectively than ever he had been by his stepfather. Clubs had been used on him – clubs and jackboots and sometimes chains and razors. Mosley's thugs had been responsible for getting Swile a long prison sentence for GBH, for Swile had hit back and almost murdered one of the blackshirt boys, and had ended up in Dartmoor. There had been some fascists as well, in the Moor; and the warders couldn't be everywhere, not all the time, and Swile had been done up more than once, and had hit back, and got his sentence prolonged while the fascists mostly seemed to get away with it.

Swile had a deep and abiding hatred of Nazis, a pathological loathing of all Germans as a result. To have one of them living in cabin luxury aboard the *Hardraw Falls* was not good. Swile went about his work with mutinous mutters, his face more closed up than ever, and a red light in his eye.

EIGHT

'Well, Petty Officer Napper. What precisely happened to you?'
Kemp had sent for Napper to report to his cabin after von Hagen
had been taken below again. Napper stood before the Commodore, at attention with his uniform cap beneath his left arm.

'Got jammed up, sir. Force o' enemy fire, sir.'

'A little more detail, I think.'

'Yessir.' Napper stared over Kemp's head, towards the square
port. 'Got flung acrorss the deck, sir, and landed up in a washport. Nearly went overboard, sir. I ended up with one leg out-
board and the other inboard, sir. If you see what I mean.'

Kemp kept a straight face. 'Like a pair of scissors?'

'You might say so, sir, yes.'

'H'm. Any damage?'

Napper said, 'It's painful, sir, very.'

'Do you need a doctor?'

'I reckon I do, sir, yes.'

Kemp cursed inwardly; he wanted no more delays at sea but
had had to ask the question and now that it had been answered
affirmatively he couldn't deny a man medical attention if it was
obtainable. He said, 'Very well, Napper, I'll make a signal to
Portree. In the meantime, although I realize you were *hors de
combat* . . .' He read the puzzlement in Napper's face and went
on, '. . . jammed in the washport at the time, you still had the responsibility for the close-range weapons. It was a pretty poor
business, Napper – to disobey the cease fire.'

'Yessir. Not my fault, sir.'

Kemp said patiently, 'I've already referred to that. If you'd
been there in person, I'd have punished you by warrant and

79

you'd have been disrated. As it was, you should have made your presence felt in advance, if you follow me. You'll see that nothing similar ever occurs again.'

'Yessir.'

'If it does, you're for the chop. As it is, I shall speak to all the guns' crews before dusk action stations. In the meantime . . . I understand it was Able Seaman Grove who was in charge aft.'

'Yessir, it was, sir. Grove, 'e's a – '

'Yes, all right, Napper. Bring him to the bridge in ten minutes' time, charged with disobedience of orders whilst in action.'

'Yessir.' Napper remained at attention.

'That's all, Napper.'

'Er. . . .' Napper cleared his throat. 'If I might refer to it again, sir – '

'Yes, the doctor. I have it in mind, Napper. I shall let you know.'

ii

Kemp had gone to town on Grove: disobedience of orders was the worst crime in action, short of deserting your gun. Kemp had quoted the Naval Discipline Act and the Articles of War and Grove had prepared himself for the worst – or not quite the worst, because the Articles of War prescribed death as the ultimate penalty to be exacted and that he didn't expect – and had been vastly astonished to be let off with a caution, which confirmed him in his view that Kemp, notwithstanding all the brass on his sleeves and cap, was a sight more human than bloody Napper. Leaving the Commodore's presence, however, Grove felt a strong sense of grievance that he'd been hauled up at all. Somebody didn't seem to know there was a war on; wasn't it a gunner's job to kill Nazis? Why show them any humanity? Kemp should have let the guns' crews alone. Apart from anything else, the Nazis were better off dead from gunfire than freezing in the hogwash. Grove had an inner certainty that bloody Napper had put in a bad word on his behalf and the Commodore was duty bound to act.

So sod Napper. . . . Making his way aft from the bridge, Grove's face widened in a big grin. He'd got a bollocking from

80

Kemp all right, but Napper, according to the buzz, had now got bollocked-up bollocks from his fight with the washport. Ever since, the PO had been walking about the decks looking as if he'd had a nasty accident in his pants.

Currently Petty Officer Napper's misfortune was causing concern on the bridge: Kemp had a word with Cutler.

'Bit of a hypochondriac, isn't he, Cutler?'

'You can say that again, sir.'

'I don't want to say it again. I've just said it.'

'Sorry, sir,' Cutler said cheerfully. 'I'm just a goddam Yank. But Petty Officer Napper – you were asking. Always got something the matter, but this time I guess he's real sore where it matters. Or could matter to his old lady.'

Kemp blew out a long breath, irritated that he should have to concern himself and ultimately the convoy with anyone's sex life, which didn't exist at sea. He said, 'Oh, very well, make a signal to *Portree*, then ... ask for their medico to advise by lamp.'

'Yes, sir. He'll want some technical information to go on, won't he?'

'I suppose so. Oh, damn it, Cutler – balls caught in a washport, it's simple enough! If you want to put it in a more medical form, have a word with Corrigan – I understand he was a medical student.'

iii

By now the main body of the PQ convoy was beginning its approach to the North Cape and the bitter weather that would meet the ships as they turned easterly between Spitzbergen and Norway's far north to enter the Barents Sea and then the White Sea for Archangel. Already the decks were icing up and to move about them was little short of suicidal; even the lifelines were strings of ice along which the heavily gloved hands of the seamen slid without hindrance. The fo'c'sle gear was frozen solid, the cables and slips set in ice deposited as the sea and spray froze almost on impact. Before arrival, the crews would be set to chip away the ice in a probably forlorn attempt to beat the weather and free the anchors. Currently only the guns were usable, kept free of ice by their crews working constantly to maintain their defence against anything Hitler might decide to throw at them. There was a curious feeling throughout all the ships, both escort and merchantmen: true, there had already been casualties – two more ships lost, and the Commodore still out of contact which might mean anything ... but the full weight of the enemy appeared to have been held off and that in itself was worrying: the general feeling was that something was being stored up – either that, or Hitler had missed the bus, which wasn't likely. There was also a lack of information from the Operations Room at the Admiralty; that could only mean that the Admiralty was as much in the dark as were the ships at sea. There was normally some indication coming through as to the likely movements of the U-boat packs or the surface vessels, the latter only too eager to attack the convoys eastward of the North Cape when they thought they were safe on the last leg into Murmansk or Archangel. Hitler's naval arm was a long one, as was his air arm.

Rear-Admiral Fellowes was concerned about the Commodore. For the tenth time that early morning he walked into the after part of *Nottingham*'s bridge and scanned the sea astern. It stood empty, bleak; once again there was a hint of snow to come. Fellowes lowered his binoculars and spoke to his Flag Captain. 'The pick-up,' he said. 'Something gone wrong I shouldn't wonder. Or the German was simply late.'

'The *Hardraw Falls* herself – '

'Yes, she could have met trouble, of course. I don't like it.'

'Nothing we can do, sir.'

'No. Just steam on. That's what I don't like ... leaving Kemp to it. Damn it, I can't even slow the convoy! Any day now, Archangel's going to ice up.'

'It was always on the cards we might have to enter Murmansk, sir.'

Fellowes nodded but didn't comment. At the moment the orders were for Archangel and he had to make it in time for the homeward convoy to get out of the port before the ice blocked the entry channel. For some reason the Russians were set on Archangel; and Fellowes saw the German agent as the obvious explanation for that.

82

iv

'*Portree* calling, sir.' Corrigan read off the lamp flashing from the destroyer's bridge. 'From the surgeon lieutenant, sir: "Please indicate if there is blood in urine."'

'Damn!' Kemp said. 'Cutler, send down for Petty Officer Napper. Or better still, go yourself and ask him.'

Cutler gave a cough and a sideways nod. 'How about Corrigan, sir?'

'Corrigan? Oh – yes. Good idea! Corrigan, you have a medical background. Get your relief up and go and check the details with Petty Officer Napper.'

'Aye, aye, sir.' Corrigan went to the voice-pipe connecting with the naval mess and blew down it. The relief signalman came to the bridge and Corrigan left on his errand of mercy. When he returned he reported that Napper had found no trace of blood.

'Thank you, Corrigan. Make that to *Portree*.'

Corrigan did so; another signal was flashed across within a few minutes: 'Watch and report size of affected part. Medical attention should not be necessary if swelling does not increase.'

'Right,' Kemp said. 'See that Napper is informed of that, Cutler. It'll be up to him to report immediately if – er – '

'If his balls reach balloon size, sir.'

'There's no need to be crude,' Kemp said. The message went down to Petty Officer Napper, who scowled and said the bloody quack should try suffering a similar disability and see how he liked it. There ought to be some sort of treatment to ease the pain, but was the quack going to be bothered? Oh, no! Sit on his arse. ... Napper couldn't do even that comfortably since what the quack so delicately called the affected part was so bloody big he couldn't avoid sitting bang on it, which meant he'd have to stand till doomsday. Muttering to himself, Napper ferreted about in his medical stockpile and found a tube of lanolin ointment.

Lanolin might help. It was worth a try. Napper went along to the heads and annointed the affected part. Afterwards he was horribly greasy but the lanolin seemed to have cooled it down.

83

'Coming up to the North Cape,' Theakston said, after a look at the chart. 'We should raise it within an hour.'

Kemp nodded. 'Just before dark. Still no convoy.'

'They can't be far ahead.'

'I wish to God,' Kemp said, 'we could break wireless silence! I've got that ice in mind. The convoy might enter Murmansk, and if we haven't caught up, we'll never know.'

'We can make an independent decision from the weather reports, Commodore.'

'Yes. I don't want to deviate – but I may be forced to, of course. I take it your chart's fully corrected for the approaches to Murmansk?'

Theakston answered stiffly. 'You have no need to ask.'

'My apologies, Captain. I was merely going on to say that my own folio's at your disposal if you need it.'

'Thank you. I'll have no need of that.'

Kemp felt severely rebuked. He remained on the bridge until the North Cape was raised on the starboard bow as dusk was setting in and stayed on until after dusk action stations were fallen out. Then he went below : there was work to be done, more talking with von Hagen. On the way down the ladder to the master's deck he encountered Petty Officer Napper checking on the gunners of the watch.

'Well, Napper. How's it going ? Still painful ?'

'Yes, sir, *very* painful, sir.'

'You have my sympathy. Fortunately it's not lethal.' Kemp went on his way, and Napper scowled at his retreating back in its bridge coat and duffel coat. Not lethal, no ! Not to life, anyway. On the other hand you never knew. The body was a very funny thing and its reactions couldn't be predicted. One part rubbed off on another and things could spread, currently in the sense that with swollen bollocks you walked funny, and that could affect the legs, give you lumbago perhaps, upset your spinal cord so you ended up in plaster of paris, and once let that happen and all sorts of things could go wrong through the sheer inertia of being motionless and flat. You could get obese and bugger up the heart, and your liver would go bad and what-all. Constipation would be a natural certainty, a complete gum-up, and that could lead to poisoned intestines and a sour stomach with flatulence and if you were all done up in plaster of paris you couldn't even fart. He'd best have a natter with Corrigan again. . . .

vi

Kemp said, 'We'll be in Soviet waters quite soon now, von Hagen.'

'And then after Archangel, back to England. Will the same ships go back, all of them?'

'Yes. The Russians discharge them somewhat faster than British stevedores. We sail again as soon as the holds are cleared.'

Kemp changed the subject, becoming reminiscent, talking man to man about those Australian voyages of what now seemed centuries ago, another and better life. His orders had to be obeyed : he had to milk the German of as much information as possible before he was removed by the KGB. The only way Kemp could see to do that was to get von Hagen in a reminiscent frame of mind, to talk to him of the England he had known in peacetime, the England he had come to know so well and to like. Something might penetrate, the past might be made to act upon the present and the future. Bound for all he yet knew for imprisonment in Britain, von Hagen might well see no reason not to talk to Kemp so long as he accepted that eventually he was going to be made to talk to Military Intelligence. On the other hand, of course, he might believe that even under intensive interrogation he could retain his secrets for his Führer's sake – or more likely for his own anti-communism.

They talked of persons they had both known and von Hagen talked easily enough, and anecdotally. An old friendship was there still and never mind that they stood now on opposite sides of the fence of war. There was a good deal of do-you-remember, of this and that, of the people who on various voyages had shared the Captain's table. Kemp steered the conversation towards Britain – towards London, where von Hagen had lived

85

in a service flat in Whitehall Court, with big windows looking out over the Embankment and the Thames busy with its strings of laden barges, an expensive and comfortable flat, rather on the large side for a bachelor which von Hagen was then and still remained.

'London,' von Hagen said with an inward smile. 'Yes, they were happy years and I miss them very much to be truthful. English women ... do you know, I found our German *Hausfrauen* heavy going after the English women! Yes, London was a very good place to be in those days.' He paused, eyes now holding a backward look. 'What's it like now, Commodore?'

Kemp shrugged. 'I avoid the place whenever possible. My wife likes to go up for shopping ... it's not my cup of tea. When I'm not being a seaman, I'm a countryman.' He, too, paused and rubbed reflectively at his chin. 'Of course it's terribly changed – it was bound to be. All the bombing. A good many landmarks gone and plenty of debris. And all the casualties ... but you'll know all that for yourself, von Hagen.'

'You hold me responsible.'

'Not you personally – of course not. Unless you were one of the London-domiciled German nationals who were able to be of assistance to your Intelligence services.'

Von Hagen shrugged. 'It would be foolish to deny that I was questioned. Because of friendships and old times I did my best not to be ... too helpful.'

'I'm glad to hear that. I'd like to think you might be helpful now.'

The German's eyes narrowed: he looked watchful, alert. 'Yes?'

'You have many secrets, obviously. Things that could save lives, perhaps.'

'British lives?'

'You enjoyed England once. You liked the people.'

'I think you are asking me to be a traitor, Commodore.'

Kemp gave an involuntary sigh. 'I suppose so. But you're going to be interrogated anyway. I thought perhaps ... if there was anything you'd care to tell me. ...'

'You would then put in a good word for me?'

'Something like that,' Kemp said. He looked down at his knees: he couldn't face von Hagen, but he went on, 'As an old shipmate, I might be easier to talk to. That's what I thought, anyway.'

There was a smile on von Hagen's face now and he spoke gently. 'My dear chap, you would make a very rotten agent, and a very rotten interrogator!'

'Certainly I would. I have no ambition to be either!'

'No, I would never expect it of you. And you are also very transparent. Another word would be honest.'

'Thank you.'

'And you are out of your depth. You are trying to make me talk, you are trying to deceive and because of that transparent honesty you are failing very badly.'

'Von Hagen, I – '

'You are under orders from someone who does not know you. You are being made use of. Why? Can you tell me that, my old friend Captain Kemp?' When there was no answer from Kemp the German went on, 'There is another point. I am about to enter Russian waters – we have discussed that already, of course. You will hide me, and you will permit no search of the ship by the KGB. You assured me of that. But I see a very plain connection. Please be honest with me. I think our past friendship gives me the right to that.'

Kemp got to his feet and paced the cabin, backwards and forwards, his fists clenching and unclenching. He felt the movement of the ship beneath his feet, saw the sway of the curtain across the square port – now with the deadlight secured behind it to preserve the blackout – listened to the engine sounds and the noise of the forced-draught system, all the familiarities of the sea that had been his life, a clean life lived among predominantly decent men. He felt defiled now, as though he were throwing all the past away. But the country was at war, the country was on the brink of being starved out as a result of the sustained cruelty of the war at sea, of the shattering ferocity of the attacks on the convoys – and he had his orders. Could he have the temerity to set his own feelings, his own self-estimation, against the interest of ordinary people in Britain who were enduring privation and air attack, night after night in so many of the big cities? Which came first?

He turned, and faced von Hagen. He said, 'Very well, I shall be honest. I have orders from Whitehall to get you to talk to me.

You, a top Nazi agent, must know a great deal that would be helpful.'

'Obviously, yes. But the coming interrogation by your Military Intelligence ... or is it not to come?' The German's eyes were hard now. 'I think I see it all. But please put it into words yourself, my old friend.'

Kemp scarcely recognized the sound of his own voice when he said, each word coming out painfully, 'Unless you talk fully to me, I am to hand you over to the Russians on arrival in Archangel.'

NINE

For a while there had been a silence; Kemp wished the sea would open and suck him down. Von Hagen stared at him, his face working, all colour gone from it. He said after almost a minute, 'That would be to sign my death warrant. After torture, that is. The Kremlin has wanted me for a long time.'

'I'm more sorry than I can possibly say.'

'Yes, I believe you. You are a man in a torture of his own at this moment. But tell me something more: how would you know if I told you all I know, how would you know if I was speaking the truth in what I said? Would I not say anything in order to preserve myself against the Russians, against Comrade Stalin?'

'I suppose so.'

Von Hagen laughed. 'You suppose so! And I suppose you do suppose so. What then? What use my speaking?'

'I don't know, von Hagen. I'm simply under orders and I don't even know, precisely, from whom. Whoever it is, he must know his business.'

'Of course. And now shall I tell you what you don't yet know? Shall I tell you what all my experiences of governments and politicians and persons in Intelligence lead to me to assess for certain what will happen in Archangel?'

Kemp nodded.

'You have a British naval presence in Archangel.'

'Yes. A British Naval Liaison Officer.'

'His role is not merely liaison, my friend. He will have an Intelligence officer on his staff, though the fact will be disguised under the cover of some other appointment. This officer will interrogate me before I am handed over to the Russians. He will

89

be an experienced interrogator who will find out, under threat of my hand-over, what you will not have found out. *You* are not being relied upon exclusively, you see.'

Kemp lifted his arms, let them drop again. Out of his depth was a gross understatement. He felt helpless, caught in a trap, a man being used, manipulated by unscrupulous persons. He said heavily, 'I suppose you could be right.'

'I'm certain I am. You may ask, why bother to interrogate me at all when, if I am *not* handed over to the Russians as will be promised in return for my co-operation, I can be brought after all to Britain in the homeward convoy? There is a very simple answer to that . . . isn't there?'

Kemp nodded. There was no need to put it into words: his own orders had already stipulated the hand-over come what may, the broken promise, the cynical disregard of what would happen to von Hagen. And von Hagen knew it all. The German was going on again. 'You yourself told me, you would not permit a search of your ship. But they will know already that I am aboard. You realize this?'

Kemp said, 'That's only supposition.'

'Oh, no! I know my value to the Russians, and it is plain to me now that a deal has been arranged between Whitehall and the Kremlin. You'll not have a chance to hide me away.'

'I shall do my best,' Kemp said simply.

Von Hagen smiled with a touch of sadness, almost of a kind of compassion for a man in torment. 'You will do your best . . . if I talk to you now?'

'Yes,' Kemp answered. 'My best . . . so help me God.'

Von Hagen closed his eyes and held his hands up, parson fashion, the finger-tips together, in front of his face. He could have been in prayer, Kemp thought. There was a lengthy silence in the cabin: a clock ticked loudly from the bulkhead beside the square port, and Kemp could hear the footfalls of the officer of the watch above his head, hear the occasional clatter and rasp of the telemotor steering gear as the quartermaster moved the wheel to keep the *Hardraw Falls* on course. Then at last von Hagen spoke.

He said, 'For me, the war is over – that is what they tell prisoners of war, isn't it? – whichever side takes me I am finished for Germany, and I am split between Britain and Germany. You will believe me, I hope, when I say that I've never worked against the British as such. My experience has been in Norway, against the Resistance. Except when, as I've said, I was obliged to answer certain obvious questions about London and so on ... I never went further than that.'

'I believe that,' Kemp said, but von Hagen appeared not to listen.

'Now I shall tell you two things, and two things only. I shall tell you out of friendship, because I wish no harm to come to you personally. One of these things is uncertain, the other is very certain.'

Kemp said, 'Go on, von Hagen.'

'The certain one first: there is to be a heavy attack on your convoy after it has passed the North Cape into the Barents Sea, once it is off the Kola Inlet outside Murmansk. I – '

'You knew this, knew it when you came aboard?'

Von Hagen smiled. 'Obviously! I have no concealed radio receiver – '

'But you were surprised to find the convoy was outward bound for Russia. Surprised and – worried.'

Von Hagen nodded. 'Yes. Because I could not believe I was to be taken to Russia. Up to that time, I had made the assumption your convoy was bound for the United Kingdom. When I was told differently, you see – then I knew, that it is *your* convoy that is to be attacked.' He leaned forward, eyes on Kemp's face. 'A battle fleet is lying off to the south of Spitzbergen – I can give you its composition. There are three heavy cruisers and a pocket battleship, with destroyer escorts, and more forces will leave ports in north Norway to cut off any retreat round the North Cape. Also there will be air support from the Norwegian airfields. Those are the certainties.'

'And the uncertainties?'

Von Hagen said, 'It is possible that by now it is known to our High Command that I have been taken. If they wish to get me back – '

'They'll hold off the *Hardraw Falls*? No – stupid of me! They won't know which ship you're in. Or will they, von Hagen?'

'It's possible. There was the U-boat attack, and the U-boat will have reported by w/t whilst surfaced.' It had; Kemp's leading telegraphist had reported a brief transmission. 'Two and two may be put together in Berlin – a ship detached from the convoy, off the Norwegian coast, much closer in than is normal. If, as I said, they know I've been taken – well, the rest is a simple deduction, I think.'

'Perhaps. Is there anything else you want to say?'

Von Hagen shook his head. 'I shall say no more. I shall not burden you, Captain Kemp. I am convinced I am right about your naval staff in Archangel. Let the questioning rest with them. They are not my friends.'

The German got to his feet and held out his hand. With no hesitation, Kemp took it in a firm grip. Then he called for Cutler to remove the prisoner.

ii

Kemp called a conference in his cabin: Captain Theakston and Cutler were present together with the naval telegraphist on the Commodore's staff, Leading Telegraphist Rose.

Kemp told them the apparent facts. He went on, 'The *Admiral Scheer*, with *Regensburg, Göttingen* and *Koblenz*. Pretty lethal! The convoy won't stand a chance, except perhaps if the order to scatter is given. The Rear-Admiral may decide to do just that, and then put himself and the escort between the convoy and the attack force. If he has the time. And that's up to me, I fancy.' He took a deep breath. 'I propose to break wireless silence and inform both the escort and the Admiralty.'

Cutler said, 'The Nazis'll pick up the transmission, sir.'

'Yes, they will. So?'

'So they'll move in faster. Before the British Admiralty can redeploy from – '

'That won't matter. According to von Hagen, the attack's imminent in any case. Speed's the watchword now, Cutler, no time even to cypher up a signal – '

'Plain language, sir? Why, that's against – '

'Never mind what it's against, Cutler. Rose?'

'Sir?'

'Make in plain language, from Commodore to Rear-Admiral Commanding the escort repeated Admiralty: "PQ convoy expected to come under heavy attack from Spitzbergen area at any time." Prefix Most Immediate.'

'Aye, aye, sir.' Rose, who had taken down the signal as Kemp had been speaking, left the cabin for the wireless office. Kemp turned to Theakston.

He said, 'As for us, Captain, we're likely to be something of a marked ship – because of von Hagen. We've no idea how much the Nazis know. If they're aware of the facts they may not attack to sink. But they'll try to board and hook off von Hagen.'

'Aye, and *then* sink us,' Theakston said dourly.

Kemp had all officers and senior hands off watch mustered in the saloon. He believed that secrecy would not at this stage be compromised by his taking the ship's crew into his confidence, at any rate so far as possible ; he said nothing of what was intended to happen to the prisoner if he was got as far as Archangel ; but afterwards von Hagen got the blame from the crew. Chief Steward Buckle put it succinctly.

'Best thing if the bugger was dumped overboard.'

'Induced suicide ?' Napper asked sarcastically.

'Why not ? Best way out for him, never mind us ! Bugger'll get the chop anyway, back in UK.'

'Commodore couldn't wear that,' Napper said with a sniff. 'Get himself court martialled, wouldn't he, for neglect o' duty. Come to that – so would I. PO in charge o' escort. . . .'

'And you wouldn't risk *that*, not even for the sake of the ship and all of us.'

Napper said crossly, 'O' course I bloody wouldn't.' He broke off the conversation and went aft with his curious waddling gait : in spite of the lanolin, he was no better. But measurements taken as accurately and carefully as possible had indicated no increase in the swelling. With luck there would be a subsidence by the time he got home again. If ever he did. He didn't fancy taking on what had sounded like the entire German surface fleet, even less so when he couldn't walk straight. But walk straight or walk in a twist, he knew his duty : he went conscientiously on a tour of the close-range weapons, all round the ship in the freezing, perishing cold, slithering on the iced-up decks – you never could get a decent grip with seaboots – feeling round the moving parts of the guns to make sure the ice hadn't got at them, his skin almost sticking to the metal even through his woollen gloves. Peashooters, that was what they were, but they just might stop the jerries boarding. . . .

'Able Seaman Grove – '

'Yes, PO ?'

'Wipe that grin orf your face, double quick.'

'Sorry, PO.'

'You'll be fuckin' sorrier if I sees it again.'

Grove kept a straight face until Napper had turned his back and moved on. Napper, in his view, had used an inappropriate adjective for a man in his condition. Grove found himself wondering how crabs did it.

iv

Still ahead of the *Hardraw Falls* Rear-Admiral Fellowes, muffled to the ears on the flagship's bridge, tapped the signal form that had been brought to him at the double. 'Indiscreet – very. Plain language . . . the German Naval Staff – bound to reinforce !'

'It'll make the Admiralty pull its finger out,' the Flag Captain said. He believed Kemp to have been right: out of visual touch with the Flag – what else could he have done? Encyphering would have wasted many vital minutes, decyphering would have wasted more. He repeated his remark about the Admiralty sending in heavy ships.

'Not as fast as the Germans,' Fellowes said.

That was true : if the report from the *Hardraw Falls* was accurate, the German units were very much nearer than any available British ships.

The Flag Captain asked, 'Do you intend to scatter, sir ?'

'I don't know. That's pretty extreme.' The Rear-Admiral looked around at the convoy and the shepherding escorts, shadows in the night, the night that from now on would last almost round the clock as they came into the northernmost waters of the convoy route, into the land of the midnight sun in summer, the region where in winter the *aurora borealis* was at its most spec-

94

tacular, the streaming Northern Lights spreading their colours vividly across the dark sky. The convoy would stand out beautifully beneath those great streaks of light, helpless targets for the German guns. Fellowes did a swift calculation in his head of what the Germans would produce: total gun-power something in the order of six 11-inch plus twenty-four 8-inch, plus secondary armament and anti-aircraft batteries, plus the torpedo-tubes of the destroyer escort that would be in company with the fleet. Quite a lot, and the convoy covered a lot of water.

Fellowes made up his mind. 'I'm not going to scatter. We're not all that far off Murmansk – and bugger Archangel in the circumstances.' He turned aside and called to the chief yeoman of signals.

'Chief Yeoman ... make to Captain(D), "You are to detach one destroyer with the A/S corvettes to stand by convoy into Murmansk repeat Murmansk. Heavy German force expected to make contact from Spitzbergen." Message ends. Make to the Vice-Commodore, "convoy will detach to Murmansk repeat Murmansk to avoid expected enemy attack. Executive will follow shortly."' Fellowes paused. 'One more, Chief Yeoman.'

'Aye, aye, sir.'

'To *Neath* ... and Captain(D) again: "Remaining ships will alter north-eastwards to engage the enemy."'

v

In the Operations Room in the Admiralty bunker beneath Horse Guards Parade there was a high degree of consternation when the message from Commodore Kemp came in. Nothing had been known of any enemy concentration in the waters off Spitzbergen. Heads were due to roll if Kemp's information was correct. In the meantime it had to be accepted that it was.

'We know he picked up von Hagen,' the Duty Captain said. A signal to that effect had been reported from the submarine. His face showing strain, the Duty Captain took up a red telephone and dialled a single digit. The call was answered almost immediately and the Captain made his report. He listened thereafter, saying little. When he put down the phone he got to his feet and went across to the large map that covered most of one wall, with

WRNS officers and ratings standing by with pointers to shift the cardboard silhouettes of the warships in home waters. To his deputy he said, 'Most Immediate to C-in-C Home Fleet from Chief of Naval Staff. "You are to proceed forthwith to give cover to PQ convoy off Kola Inlet and to engage heavy German force believed moving south from Spitzbergen."'

He looked again at the wall map: the 2nd Battle Squadron of the Home Fleet lay currently in Scapa Flow, a depleted force consisting of *Rodney* and the old, slow *Ramillies*; *Rodney* carrying nine 6-inch guns, *Ramillies* eight 15-inch and capable of only twenty-one knots at full stretch, a speed she couldn't hope to maintain for long if, in fact, she could make it at all. Both battleships were only just in from an Atlantic convoy escort, sea worn and with stores to replenish. The stores would have to wait. In Rosyth, also within the command of C-in-C Home Fleet, was the battle-cruiser *Renown* together with the aircraft-carrier *Victorious*. All these heavy units were accompanied by their destroyer escorts; and would leave in company with the 18th Cruiser Squadron consisting of *Sheffield*, *Edinburgh*, *Belfast* and *Newcastle*.

vi

From the bridge of the *Hardraw Falls* Kemp watched, as had Rear-Admiral Fellowes, the play of the Northern Lights as they lit the sky ahead. He felt a sudden shiver of apprehension: there was something about that amazing illumination, something primeval and awe-inspiring.

'"Fearful lights that never beckon, save when kings and heroes die" ... some poet or other wrote that, Cutler.'

'I wouldn't have thought you read poetry, sir?'

Kemp laughed. 'Think it's pansy, do you?'

'Well, sir, no, not quite that.'

'Never mind, anyway. It just came to mind.'

'Because men are going to die?'

'We won't dwell on that, Cutler.'

'No, sir.'

'We'll concentrate on a sharp lookout.'

'Not much we can do if we sight anything, sir.'

96

'Bugger all,' Kemp said with another laugh. 'Except bugger off!'

Cutler made no response to that: Kemp had already made his intentions known to all hands. They were well round the North Cape by this time and the only viable direction in which to bugger off would be for a Russian port, and the orders were still for Archangel even though Murmansk was handier. The *Hardraw Falls* had no speed to match that of the heavy Nazi units and Cutler believed they were – or would be if sighted – steaming towards oblivion. He felt somehow detached about the prospect: he'd always wanted to go to sea and he'd wanted action, and if in the course of that action he bought it, well, that would be just too bad. No use moaning, and no use trying to avoid the inevitable either. He hoped for just one thing: not yet tested in full action, he hoped he could stand up to it and not let the USA down by showing fear. If he did, there would be those – not many it was true – who wouldn't hesitate to let him know they knew: that Napper for one. Napper didn't like Yanks . . . Cutler believed he didn't like action either. There was an expression in the British Navy and it could well be applied to Petty Officer Napper: all wind and piss like the barber's cat.

And what was it like back in Texas tonight?

The rolling hills, the wide-open spaces, the big ranches far from the sea, the ice and the war in Europe . . . Tex Cutler's old man ran a ranch, not one of the biggest, but big enough by British standards, and one day Cutler, along with his two brothers, would inherit it. One day – if he lived to see it; he rather hoped he wouldn't give his father the pain of outliving a son, but even with that thought in mind he had no regrets for what might be about to happen. If he had to die, he couldn't die in better company than that of Kemp and Theakston . . . he glanced across at Theakston now, standing in the port bridge wing, head sunk beneath the hood of his duffel coat, his body motionless as if frozen to the guardrail, his steaming breath visible in opaque clouds in the glow of the Northern Lights. Theakston and Kemp – they were both like rocks of dependability, each with his own worries probably, personal family anxieties that would not intrude on the duty of either of them.

The night so far was in fact peaceful: but not for much longer, probably. And the shatter came even as Cutler had the thought:

a blue-shaded lamp winked from the bridge of the destroyer escort and Leading Signalman Corrigan reported to the Commodore.

'Surface contact, sir, bearing green four five, distant twelve miles.'

TEN

Tension had mounted throughout the ship: Sub-Lieutenant Cutler was far from being the only one aboard who saw oblivion staring the *Hardraw Falls* in the face. Below in the engine-room Chief Engineer Sparrow stood grim-faced on the starting platform, wondering, amidst his thoughts about being the target for an unknown number of heavy German gun batteries, just how long his engines were going to stand the strain of being pushed to their maximum and beyond. They were not in their first flush of youth by any means, any more than he was himself, and they'd been pushed for too long already in the Commodore's attempts to catch up with the convoy. Before long, something was likely to give. When the bridge passed down the word that there had been a surface contact, Sparrow was in no doubt what Theakston wanted: more speed.

'Not possible,' he said. 'Engines are rattling to pieces as it is.'

'Do your best, Chief,' Theakston said.

Do your best, Sparrow thought, it's the equivalent of the army's 'carry on, sergeant'. He passed the word, just for form's sake, to the second engineer, who shook his head in disbelief that the bridge could expect miracles.

'What's the Old Man think we are, eh?'

Sparrow disregarded the rhetorical question. He said, 'If this is the Jerry heavies, then I reckon they must have missed the main convoy.'

'And found us. If so, it's curtains.' Weller gave the chief one of his calculating looks. The strain of war – of being about to be blown sky-high – would likely tell. Sparrow, seeing that look, knew what it meant. But it was somewhat on the late side now, he reckoned. They'd go aloft to the pearly gates still in the relationship of chief and second engineer. And if they were to make that final trip, then Sparrow wished they would get on with it. The tension engendered by waiting for the big bang and the clouds of boiling steam was acting upon him like they said about a drowning man, all his past life flashing like a cinema screen before his eyes, some good, some bad. Home and the wife and kids, ports all over the world, runs ashore to get boozed up with his friends and then find a woman, white, yellow or black; unfaithfulness had never mattered much then but it did now. He should have been more contained and it was, he thought regretfully, too late now to put in a good word for himself, a sort of apology.

Chief Steward Buckle was feeling much the same: so far in this war he had never been so close to the enemy as to fear the worst, had never been entirely alone on the waters as the *Hardraw Falls* now was, never been the main – the only – target for a strong force who probably believed they were about to make contact with the whole convoy and its escort and would blast away with everything they had the moment the *Hardraw Falls* was sighted. Not much hope now of making a small fortune out of caviar and possibly just as well really since it would have been another shady fiddle to be chalked up against him, and God knew – and might shortly tell – how many fiddles he'd worked in the past, regarding them as chief steward's perks. He wasn't alone, of course: he had once heard a shipmaster say that you could always tell which was the chief steward when the officers and crew went ashore in a home port, out of uniform, because the chief steward would be the only one with a car.

ii

So far there had been no gunfire and there had been no identification either: their destroyer escort had made no further reports, no doubt in the interest of remaining anonymous for as long as possible, though it could be assumed the ship they had picked up on the radar would have picked them up at the same time.

'Playing possum,' Cutler said.

'It seems to be the case, but why, for God's sake?' Kemp stared ahead: the sea was far from fully dark beneath the patterns of light but he could pick up no ship. Whoever it was could not be on a closing course. Was it remaining, as it were, parallel, keeping just outside range, or was it steaming away? For the moment there was uncertainty in the air. Kemp said, 'It could be an arse-end Charlie from the convoy, I suppose.'

After another five minutes *Portree* was seen to be calling up again. Corrigan reported, 'Contact moving north-west now lost, sir.'

'Thank you, Corrigan. Keep the guns' crews closed up, Cutler.' Kemp glanced at Theakston standing by his side. 'This is a mystery, Captain. There's a possible solution ... it could be the Rear-Admiral doing what I thought he might – moving to put himself between the convoy and the German units. *Portree* could have got an echo off one on the extended screen.'

'Sounds likely,' Theakston said.

Kemp turned away and paced the bridge, back into the interminable business of awaiting developments, of trying to foresee the unforeseeable, of attempting to get into other men's minds and act ahead of them. *Would* one of the objectives of the German warships be to get von Hagen back? There was no absolute certainty on that score, and in fact the German naval command would scarcely commit so many heavy ships to that purpose, surely? An all-out attack on the convoy must be presumed to be the first priority. If that was so, should he, Kemp, be in duty bound to stand clear and not force the speed in his attempt to catch up? The *Hardraw Falls* would add nothing to the defence of the convoy, that was for sure. Just another target – and he had that valuable cargo.

Valuable to whom? The answer to that was principally the Russians, and Kemp was determined to do what he could to honour his promise to von Hagen, the promise that he would do his best for him. Even so, he couldn't go against his orders. Von Hagen, it seemed, was an important element in the current game of chess being played between two governments. . . .

Kemp went into the chartroom and looked at the chart spread open on the wide mahogany table with pointers, set squares and parallel rulers laid neatly on top of it. The course for Archangel was marked in pencil from the last fix: near enough six hundred miles to go, but only three hundred and seventy to the entry to the White Sea and safety from German surface attack if not a daring *Luftwaffe* – around thirty hours' steaming. Murmansk lay nearer, some two hundred miles distant – the *Hardraw Falls* could make the port inside some sixteen hours.

But the orders were still for Archangel. No doubt the scene had been set there, all preparations made for an act of betrayal. Or could you ever be said to betray the enemy? Perhaps not.

Kemp left the chartroom, went back into the cold of the open bridge. The wind was keener than ever, and everywhere on deck the ice had tightened its grip. There was no evidence of any other ship. Not yet; but the German force would presumably be sweeping south to engage.

iii

Petty Officer Napper had gone below to the heads and when he emerged he all but bumped into the chief steward. Buckle said, 'Just the man.'

'Eh?'

'Got something for you, if you've got the time.'

'Should be on deck. What is it?'

'Book on medical matters.'

'*Medical*? Yes, I got the time.'

Napper went with Buckle to the latter's office. Buckle produced a volume: *The Ship Captain's Medical Guide*. 'Skipper sent down for it after you got – what you got. Couldn't bloody find it, not then. But it's turned up.'

'Thanks a lot,' Napper said eagerly. The book should prove a mine of information.

'Page 176, testicles,' Buckle said.

Napper flipped through the pages and found the relevant entry and his eyes widened as he read and an expression of indignation spread across his face. Bloody quacks! The doc in the *Portree* – ought to be struck off. The treatment stared Napper in the face: a man with bruised bollocks should be given bed rest and the testicles supported with a pillow. There was even a picture of it, the part all swollen up like a melon, resting on the prescribed pillow.

He should have been put on the sick list, off all duties. As it was, he hadn't even been put on light duty, had just had to carry on. Agitatedly, Napper sucked at a hollow tooth, his face all creased up. It wasn't right, but not much use going to the bridge to complain, not just now anyway, not with the enemy around. Napper, just come from the heads, had carried out a further examination of the affected part. It wasn't any better but it wasn't any worse either, he had to admit that to himself, pillow or no pillow. He went back on deck, still moving awkwardly, and made his way to the bridge for another check on the close-range weapons, making sure the gunners had kept them ice free: in current temperatures they could ice up in seconds, almost. He exaggerated his crab-like gait when he saw the Commodore's eye on him: propaganda wasn't the province of Dr Goebbels alone.

'Petty Officer Napper. . . .'

'Yessir?'

'Contact's been lost for now. But keep the guns at full readiness and the hands alert.'

'Aye, aye, sir.' The corners of Napper's mouth turned down; Kemp hadn't noticed a bloody thing! Napper saw Leading Signalman Corrigan standing by with his Aldis lamp. Talk about useless . . . surely to God even a makee-learn quack ought to know about pillows! It really made a man sick, the way nobody cared. As soon as he got the opportunity he would write a long letter home, unburdening himself on the wife. He always felt better after a good moan.

iv

'Gunfire,' Kemp said, and brought up his binoculars to cover the port quarter. There had been a heavy rumble: big guns in action. Kemp said, 'Only one answer, Cutler.'

'The escort, sir? The main convoy escort?'

Kemp nodded briefly. 'We can't be far off the convoy. The escort's engaging the heavy German ships. Giving the convoy a chance . . . like Kennedy in the *Rawalpindi*, only with more hope of success.'

'Takes guts,' Cutler said.

'It's what they're there for.'

'Sure, but that doesn't – '

'I don't deny the guts, Cutler.'

Kemp's tone had been sharp; the American glanced up at the Commodore's set face and made a diagnosis: Kemp was feeling he wasn't doing what he himself was there for, which was taking charge of the merchant ships in convoy, acting as the rallying point. It wasn't his fault but he was blaming himself. Cutler had an idea Kemp ought to turn away, turn right away around the North Cape and head for Iceland or home waters in order to pre-serve von Hagen from the Nazis. He could always be negotiated as between the British and the Russians at a more propitious time, a case perhaps of better late than never.

Taking a chance even though he knew what the answer would be, Cutler put the point to the Commodore. Kemp reacted badly.

'I'll do no such thing, Cutler. Bugger von Hagen – my job's to overtake the convoy and get 'em into Archangel! If we're right about the escort's movements, if they've detached to take the German fire, the merchant ships are on their own now.'

'I guess so, sir,' Cutler said, but wondered what difference it would make whether or not the *Hardraw Falls* caught up. Kemp seemed to sense what was in his assistant's mind and said some-thing about the absolute necessity for leadership, of one man to make the decisions and give the orders. Meanwhile the heavy rumbles were continuing, a massive volume of sound that went on and on, menacing, a harbinger of what might be about to come to the *Hardraw Falls*. In every part of the ship men were listening, speculating, wondering what their own chances might be. One shell, if it took the ship anywhere near the holds, would finish off every man aboard as the HE went up in a shattering blast. They felt on the very verge of hell: any man who was blas-ted overboard instead of being killed outright would freeze within a minute. In the engine-room Sparrow was now straining everything in the interest of maximum speed, just hoping that nothing would give. The gunfire was reverberating even through the engine spaces: it couldn't be all that far off. The moment the Nazis had them in their sights, they would have had it. Sparrow hoped Kemp and Theakston knew what they were doing: he knew all about the German, von Hagen, or anyway as much as the galley wireless had revealed, which Sparrow realized was not likely to be the full story and doubtless inaccurate at that. But the Nazi agent must obviously be of value to the British war effort or they wouldn't have diverted the *Hardraw Falls* to pick him up . . . and come to that, why hadn't that submarine simply carried him on to a UK port? There was something extra in the air and it was to do with von Hagen.

On deck Petty Officer Napper was having similar thoughts, vengefully: if only they could ditch von Hagen, who was acting the perishing Jonah in Napper's view. If it hadn't been for him, they would have been with the convoy; and there was a degree of safety in numbers. At the very least they would have been just one target among many, while as it was they would stand out like a curate in a nudist colony. Napper reckoned that any minute now all the gun-power of the German fleet was going to be deployed against him.

'What d'you reckon, eh?'

Napper whirled about, startled. The bosun had crept up on him unawares. Napper told him what he reckoned. 'Big stuff, not a hope.'

'I don't know so much. If they know that Nazi's aboard us, I don't reckon they'll sink us.'

'Not right off, no – maybe. On the other hand, they might. Just to make bloody certain the Nazi don't give anything away. That's the important thing, to them. Stands to reason, does that.'

'If anything does,' Tawney agreed.

Napper cocked an eye. 'Meaning?'

'Proper shower, they are not much *reason* about them. The Nazis.'

'Efficient, though. Not so many bloody cock-ups as the buggers in Whitehall – or the barrack stanchions sitting on their arses in Pompey.' Napper was still aggrieved, more so than ever in fact, about his draft chit to sea. A former barrack stanchion himself, he was, like the man who suddenly finds religion, completely anti in his views of his erstwhile mates.

v

'Ship, sir, bearing red one eight five. Can't identify yet, sir.'

'Right.' Kemp's binoculars came up on the bearing. All he found was a blur. 'See anything, Cutler?'

'Just an outline, sir, distant.'

A moment later the escorting destroyer was seen to be altering course towards the bearing, heeling over sharply and increasing speed. '*Portree*'s picked it up,' Cutler said.

Kemp nodded. He was about to advise Theakston to turn away and increase the distance when there was a brilliant orange flash from the unidentified vessel and seconds later a rush of air across the bridge indicated the effectiveness of what was presumably German gunfire. Hard on the heels of the firing, a signal lamp was seen to be flashing from the unknown warship.

ELEVEN

'Well?' Kemp was impatient, feeling a surge of blood through his body: he had already made a good guess at what the signal would be.

Corrigan said, 'He's calling *Portree*, sir – '

'Can you read it?'

'Yes, sir.' Corrigan paused. '*Portree*'s being told to heave to.' There was another pause. 'Colonel von Hagen's to be made available, sir.'

'Or we'll be blown out of the water, I suppose!'

'Sort of, sir.' Corrigan added, 'He's giving us five minutes, sir.'

'I see. For now, we ignore the signal.' Kemp brought up his binoculars again: now he could see the outline of the German, a heavy cruiser, no doubt the *Regensburg*, the *Göttingen* or the *Koblenz*. She was coming in fast, but as Kemp watched she slowed. So far there had been no reaction from the *Portree* but a moment later the destroyer began calling the Commodore.

'Asking for orders, sir,' Corrigan reported.

'Make: "Hold off for the time being and maintain speed."' Kemp paced the bridge, watched by Cutler and Captain Theakston. Corrigan, the signal made, waited for further orders. Kemp, he knew, was in a massive dilemma: you didn't surrender without a fight. But there was the German agent, and in that respect the Commodore would obviously have certain orders, though Corrigan didn't know what they might be. They might not, in fact, cover a situation such as this.

And Kemp knew they did not. He had to make his own decision for good or ill. And he had to make it fast, though he doubted if the German cruiser would open fire at the end of the five minutes. They wouldn't want to blast von Hagen out of existence. He would keep them hanging on, uncertain of the British reaction. Kemp turned in his pacing to find himself confronted by the ship's master. Theakston's face was set into formidable lines and he began without preamble.

'I don't know what you propose doing, Commodore, but I know what I intend to do.'

'And that is?'

'Not to be buggered about by any Nazi agent. I'm not concerned what happens to him – '

'Perhaps not, Captain, but I have to be. He has to be got into Archangel.'

'Aye! That's the orders. I have my ship to consider. My ship, my crew, and my cargo. It's a vital cargo. The German has the whip hand, Commodore Kemp. We have to let von Hagen go across – '

'We'll keep them on a string, Captain.' Kemp looked at the luminous dial of his wrist-watch. Three minutes had now passed. The next two minutes seemed to fly away, while the *Hardraw Falls* moved on and Kemp wrestled with his decision. Obviously there could be no hope of engaging the German successfully; *Portree* carried nothing heavier then 4.7-inch guns. But Kemp was in no doubt that Whitehall considered von Hagen of more importance to the conduct of the war than the men or cargo aboard the *Hardraw Falls*. Once again he tried to see into distant, political minds, the brains of the men responsible for the overall strategy. Would it be a better thing, in their view, that von Hagen should die with the rest rather than be returned to Germany?

The answer was a clear yes. The *Hardraw Falls* had to be the sacrifice.

Kemp was about to give his decision when the German began calling again, this time addressing the *Hardraw Falls* direct. Corrigan read off the signal: 'From the German, sir, who's still not giving her signal letters. "You have a passenger who is at once to be put aboard me. You will heave-to". Message ends, sir.'

'Message as before, more or less.'

'Yes, sir.'

Kemp caught Theakston's eye. Theakston said firmly. 'We

must do as he asks. I said before, I don't give nowt for a dirty Nazi spy. I'll not hazard my ship for that.'

'I shall not part with von Hagen, Captain.'

Theakston blew out a long breath of exasperation. 'See sense! Your personal problem would be solved – no broken promise, no dirt done – '

'I can't allow that to weigh. You know that as well as I do. And there's another point, Captain. The moment von Hagen's put aboard the German, we'll be sunk by gunfire. They'll never let your cargo go free.'

Theakston said, 'That need not happen. Von Hagen is your friend, and he ranks high in Germany. He'll not let that happen. You'll have saved him from the Russians, from the KGB.'

'I'm sorry, Captain. I have my orders.'

'And I have my ship,' Theakston said doggedly. That is my responsibility, Commodore Kemp. I, too, am under orders – to reach Archangel with my cargo. *I* command the ship, you don't. In effect you're no more than a passenger.' All Theakston's Yorkshire obstinacy had surfaced now, and he stood four-square on his own bridge. 'If necessary I have the authority to place *passengers* in restraint – as you had in the liners.'

Theakston turned away and went into the wheelhouse. Kemp saw him go to the engine-room telegraph and haul the lever over to stop. He was, strictly, within his rights; and Kemp could appreciate his point of view, would probably in Theakston's place have taken up a similar position. British seamen were at immediate risk now. But von Hagen was a catch; his knowledge, if he could be made to talk – even to the Russians – could possibly shorten the war. Kemp turned away and went down the ladder to his cabin, where he unlocked the safe. When he returned to the bridge he had his revolver in his hand.

ii

The Home Fleet in Scapa and the Firth of Forth had been at immediate notice for steam and no time had been lost in proceeding to sea in accordance with the orders from the Admiralty, on course for the vicinity of the North Cape with paravanes streamed from the bows against possible mines. The battle squadron pushed through wind-blown waters at its best speed, covered by the cruisers and the extended destroyer escort. The distance would be around 1350 miles: some fifty-eight hours' steaming. The estimation was that although they would have no hope of making their arrival in time to save the PQ convoy, they would catch the heavy German units either to the north as they retreated towards Spitzbergen or to the south as they tried to escape back to their bases in occupied Norway – there was no knowing yet what the German choice would be. The Vice-Admiral commanding the battle squadron believed that it would be the latter; the Germans, their work done on the convoy, would wish to scuttle south for shelter as fast as possible. For now the Fleet steamed in two watches, half the armament manned for action, and full alertness throughout on the part of the watchkeepers on the bridges and at the lookout positions as the Fleet came north to leave Iceland on the port quarter, moving into the bitter cold and the great freeze that had gripped the convoy, the gunners' mates, the armourers and the electrical artificers constantly checking for ice in the working parts of the big gun-batteries and secondary armament.

In the Admiralty's Operations Room the counters were moved north, following the dead-reckoning estimation of the Fleet's advance. The position of the PQ convoy and its escort had now, also by dead reckoning, been moved along past the North Cape towards Archangel. The atmosphere was tense, made worse by the presence of the Prime Minister, always an unpredictable and uncomfortable person, his face pugnacious now behind the immense cigar. Beside him was the First Sea Lord, Chief of the Naval Staff.

The cigar was removed and waved in the air.

'What are the chances, First Sea Lord?'

'Slim, sir – of being of any assistance to the convoy. A question of speed. If only we had more of the KG5 class – '

'Yes. I did my best before war came, as I warned everyone it would.' The Prime Minister's face became for a moment cherubic. 'I prodded and prodded and I confess I much enjoyed the discomfiture and indeed the *exasperation* of the prodded, the wretched fellows who put votes before country. I found that Tories could be most remarkably dense, unable to see a day ahead, much less the more distant future. Yes, had they listened, we would have had enough warships.' The cigar was once again thrust back between the full lips. 'The *jackal* of Germany would never have dared to risk a fight with us in the first place if we'd rearmed in time.' For a few moments Churchill glowered towards the wall map, watching the trim figures of the Wrens with their pointers. 'That *Narzi* agent . . . which ship was he transferred to?'

'The *Hardraw Falls*, Prime Minister, an ammunition ship.'

'Ah yes. The Commodore's ship. Commodore Kemp – am I not right?'

'Yes, Prime Minister . . . if you remember, it was because he had known von Hagen that – '

'Yes, yes, I don't need reminding of everything, thank you, Admiral, I'm not in my dotage yet. Now then: what do you suppose Commodore Kemp will do if the convoy encounters the Germans? As to the Narzi agent, I mean.'

'Simply carry on, Prime Minister. What else would he do?'

'That's what I asked you.' The Prime Minister shifted irritably in his chair. 'We must not neglect the possibility that the Narzis know where von Hagen is. In that case – '

'Unlikely, sir.'

'So are many things, but the unlikelihood didn't stop them happening. I hope Commodore Kemp can be relied upon! The safe delivery of von Hagen in Archangel is paramount . . . at this stage of the war we dare not upset that arch villain Comrade Stalin, much as I would enjoy so doing.' Mr Churchill removed his cigar and aimed it like a gun at the Chief of Staff. 'That last remark goes no farther than yourself, First Sea lord.'

'Of course not, Prime Minister.'

iii

Returning to the bridge, Kemp had seen that the destroyer escort had slowed as the way came off the *Hardraw Falls* and was standing off to port, keeping herself between the Commodore's ship and the enemy cruiser. Kemp went into the wheelhouse, where the master was standing beside the engine-room telegraph.

Hearing Kemp's entry, Theakston swung round. He saw Kemp's revolver.

'What's the idea?' he asked.

'A few pot shots of my own,' Kemp answered: he had read in Theakston's face that the master fancied he was about to take over the ship himself by force of arms. The idea had flitted through Kemp's mind but only as an expression of his frustration at Theakston's obstinacy, something he would have liked to do had it been practicable, which it would not. But the fact of Theakston having taken the way off his ship had given Kemp an idea and for what it might be worth he intended to put it into effect. He said, 'The German's stopping too. Any moment now, he'll be lowering a seaboat.'

As he spoke, a searchlight came on aboard the German cruiser and its beam steadied blindingly on the bridge of the *Hardraw Falls* before moving aft. When his vision had been restored Kemp saw in the backglow of the beam that a boat was already being lowered to the cruiser's waterline ready for slipping, a boat with armed seamen aboard.

Theakston asked, 'What do you intend doing?'

'I intend to to take full advantage of a cruiser that's lying stopped – that's all!'

'What the heck – ' Theakston was looking puzzled.

Kemp said, 'That boatload's going to get a reception they're not expecting.' He raised his voice through the wheelhouse door to the open bridge. 'Corrigan!'

'Yes, sir.' Corrigan came across, the lead of his Aldis trailing behind him.

'Call up *Portree*. Tell 'em, do as I do.'

'"Do as I do", sir?'

'Yes. I doubt if that'll convey anything much to the German. And add, "fish".'

Corrigan stared. '"Fish", sir? Just that?'

'Yes. Torpedoes, man, torpedoes!'

Corrigan appeared to tick over. 'Aye, aye, sir,' he said, and doubled away to the bridge wing. Soon after the signal had been made Kemp saw the destroyer using her engines to come up more on the German's beam: *Portree*'s captain had, it seemed, cottoned on nicely. Kemp turned once more to Theakston. He would, he said, open fire on the seaboat as soon as it was within range. To Petty Officer Napper, who had come to the bridge for instructions, he said his own revolver shot was to be considered the order for all the close-range weapons to open, and they would be joined by the guns aboard *Portree*.

'Touch and go, sir,' Napper said, standing bandy-legged like a jockey. There was a stirring in his stomach: if you looked on the bright side, which in fact Napper never did, action was a good cure for constipation. But at the moment all he felt was fear. They could never bring it off, not within range of the Jerry's heavy batteries, 8-inch probably, they'd just go up like a firework, and nowhere safe to hide from it. Kemp, he reckoned, must have gone clean round the bend, like Harpic. . . .

Shaking like a jelly, Napper left the bridge and went round the gun positions, passing the orders in a voice he scarcely recognized as his own. Able Seaman Grove also seemed to find the tone a shade different, sort of high and squeaky like a eunuch, and remarked upon it, cheekily.

'Something not dropped, PO?' Grove, like Napper, believed they'd had it now and giving lip to a petty officer didn't seem dangerous any more. 'Or just dropped off, p'raps.'

'Just shut it, Grove.' Napper went away, all his spirit gone, not bothering to talk about charges of impertinence. He was wondering if he would actually feel anything in the split second during which life might linger after the explosion of the thousands of tons of HE below the hatches fore and aft – terrible agony as the soul parted from the cindered flesh and the powdered bone and wafted away on the upsurge, blown this way and that until it found anchorage on a bloody cloud somewhere. Or did you just snuff it, and pass into total oblivion, not even knowing you were dead or even that you'd ever lived at all? As a small boy Petty Officer Napper had been in the habit of lighting matches beneath garden spiders in their webs, and watching them crisp up and curl into dead husks – that came back very vividly indeed and he saw himself in a few minutes' time like those spiders, and he offered up a prayer that he might be forgiven for what he'd done to them.

Then, as he came for'ard from the after-gun position above the engineers' accommodation, the action started up around him.

As soon as the seaboat came within range of the Oerlikons, Kemp fired the single revolver-shot. He had a moment in which to see, on the fringe of the searchlight beam, the boat's crew check the rhythm of their oars as panic set in. Then the close-range weapons opened, spattering the water around the seaboat and colandering the crew. At the same time *Portree* opened with her main armament and Kemp saw the sudden flare of orange flame on the German's superstructure as some of the shells took her, and the searchlight died.

'Caught nicely with her pants down! If *Portree's* on the ball with her tin fish – ' Kemp broke off. From the port side of the destroyer there had been a puff of smoke visible beneath the Northern Lights and then a series of splashes that raised enough spray to be seen in Kemp's binoculars. The torpedoes were away and they hadn't far to go. If the torpedo-gunner's mate aboard the *Portree* knew his job those fish could hardly miss on their track towards a ship lying stopped without a hope of getting under way in time, and even if she did move, *Portree* could surely be relied upon to have given the torpedoes a nice spread, one ahead, one astern, two slap bang amidships – something like that. Just a single hit ought to be enough to slow her at the very least, give the *Hardraw Falls* time to make off at full speed and try to dodge the heavy gunfire.

Cutler came up beside the Commodore. 'Looks good, sir.'

'We won't count any chickens, Cutler.'

'No, sir, Commodore.'

Kemp noted the backsliding in the form of address but let it pass. By this time Theakston had his ship under way again, his engines coming up to full and the foam from the bow's thrust already surging aft to join the curfuffle of the screw. Just as Kemp was wondering when the German was going to react, she opened in a thunderous roar with flashes of brilliant light along her decks. There was a whistling sound close overhead and the men on the bridge ducked instinctively. Standing again Kemp saw the destroyer moving fast, twisting and turning, but maintaining a mean course straight for the German cruiser, obviously in an attempt to draw the enemy fire away from the Commodore's ship, all her for'ard guns firing. She steamed through a hail of shells, so far without damage: Kemp fancied the German gunners could have been thrown into confusion by the sudden shift of events.

Then there was a huge explosion: one at least of *Portree's* torpedoes had hit. The cruiser listed heavily. Kemp saw a great sheet of flame and felt the heat wafting back on the wind, accompanied by a feeling of pressure, of concussion. In the flame he had seen fragmented metal flying up into the sky, and bodies too. Some of the guns were firing yet, pumping away at the destroyer, leaving the *Hardraw Falls* alone for the time being. More of the *Portree's* shells were finding their marks, and through his binoculars Kemp saw the German's after funnel looking like a sieve. Smoke streamed everywhere, thick and black, beginning to obscure the cruiser's outline. Then the German gunners laid spot on to their target and in a terrible uprush of fire and fury *Portree's* bridge vanished as though it had never been. Kemp watched in horror as the destroyer's bows started to pay off to starboard: the wheelhouse would have gone up with the bridge, the ship was no longer under command. A fraction of a second later something took the fo'c'sle and both the for'ard guns joined the bridge in a tearing crescendo of sound and leaping flame. Kemp saw men running blindly along the decks, and then very suddenly the end came. There was a shattering explosion from inside the ship – most likely the fore magazine – and the fo'c'sle split away from just before the midship superstructure and vanished beneath the water, to be followed with amazing speed by the rest of the vessel, her stern lifting high until the sea entered her broken hull and took her down.

In a hoarse voice Cutler said, 'There's men in the water. . . .'

'Yes, I know.'

'You're not going to pick them up?'

'No,' Kemp said. He wiped sweat from his face with the back of a gloved hand: it crackled as he did so, starting already to freeze as it left the pores of his skin. Anyone in the water would be dead from the cold already, surely. But Kemp saw Cutler's face, a picture of blame and accusation and a kind of horrified disbelief. They had been into this before and Kemp found no words now to go over it again – the urgent need to keep the vital cargo intact for Russian use, to preserve a ship that would make a trip like this again and again if she were lucky, the need to keep von Hagen alive and out of German hands. To have stopped engines now would not have been merely to put all that at risk: it would have been a stupid act of recklessness. There was little point in trying to rescue men only to have them blown to strips of bloody flesh the moment the German landed a shell anywhere near the ammunition-filled holds of the *Hardraw Falls*.

Kemp turnd away and went towards the wheelhouse. Theakston had the engine-room telegraph at full. Catching Kemp's eye he said, 'Getting the hell out?'

'Right – we are! Put her on a zig-zag course, Captain. The German's in difficulties, but she'll still try to get us.'

'Aye, no doubt she will.'

Abruptly Kemp said, 'Those men – in the water. God damn this bloody war!'

'Aye,' Theakston said again. 'But remember this – you had no alternative. Not unless you were a lunatic.' He stared ahead through the wheelhouse screen, into the half-darkness beneath the Northern Lights still streaming across the sky. 'We who go to sea – ' He broke off as once again the sound of gunfire cut through the night. 'There she goes again, Commodore.'

'Can you squeeze out any more speed?'

Theakston gave a harsh laugh. 'My chief engineer knows what's going on. He'll need no prodding. He has what you might call a vested interest.'

'Of course. I'm sorry.' Kemp moved out again into the bridge wing, into the bitter cold, the cold that entered the body like a knife-thrust. More wind had come up, a bitter east wind from Novaya Zemlya, and there was, Kemp believed, a hint of more snow to come. If it came on the wings of that bitter wind, it would be a real blizzard through which the ships would steam blind. Meanwhile the German was firing again but erratically: Kemp believed the gunnery control system had been thrown out, that the cruiser was in gunlayer's firing. And Theakston's zig-zag course was helping too.

Kemp looked astern at the cruiser. She was now stopped and there was a curious glow that seemed to be coming from behind her plates: she appeared to be on the point of blowing up. But then, as Kemp stared through his binoculars, the *Hardraw Falls* swung on the port leg of the zig-zag and a final shot from the doomed cruiser found its target. There was a blast from for'ard, hot air that swept up and back over the bridge, and the ship's way checked suddenly, throwing men off balance. Kemp staggered, almost fell, and was caught by Cutler.

'Hit on the bow, sir!'

Kemp heard Theakston's voice, passing the orders to the chief officer to sound round, calling the engine-room on the voice-pipe. The *Hardraw Falls* moved on, a little down now by the head. Kemp prayed that the damage might be small; and gave thanks that the shell hadn't struck near the cargo holds.

v

Petty Officer Napper had gone for a burton once again, skidding on his backside along the after well-deck, but this time suffering no damage. He had a furtive feel to assure himself of this, delving beneath his duffel coat and into his waistband. He had just finished doing this when, looking aft towards the Nazi cruiser, he had a full and perfect view of what happened next. The glow that Kemp had seen from the bridge increased suddenly to extreme brilliance, almost white heat, just for a moment, a split second, and then the cruiser blew up, just like that. The whole sky and the sea for miles around lit like day and an enormous volume of sound crashed across the water and she was gone in flying metal fragments and bits of bodies that could be seen while the flame lasted, arms spread like dolls flung into the air by some wilful child, then nothing but a pall of smoke to mark where the warship had been.

'Bloody hell,' Napper said aloud. He was badly shaken up: you didn't see sights like that in Pompey barracks and in the last war Napper hadn't seen any action either, joining only at the tail end. His legs felt like a blancmange, and he hung on to a lifeline for support. Poor sods ... but of course they were only Jerries who had been trying to do something similar to himself. Napper steadied: serve the buggers right, it did. And the *Hardraw Falls* might be safe, anyway for now – so long as the damage from that shell hadn't been too great, that was. Napper shook again and muttered to himself: if they had to abandon and drift about the Barents Sea in an open boat it could be just as fatal as being blown up – and a bloody sight more lingering. And – Napper strongly suspected – all because of that there Nazi agent.

TWELVE

Chief Officer Amory came to the bridge to report to the master.

'Bows opened up, sir, bosun's store and forepeak gone, but the collision bulkhead's holding.'

'You're shoring up, I take it, Mr Amory?'

'Yes, sir. As I said, the bulkhead's holding but I can't say for how long. It'll be a question of speed and weather now.'

'Aye.' Theakston had already reduced speed to half; he and Kemp were both reluctant to reduce further but the collision bulkhead itself would have to be the deciding factor. 'I'll come down for'ard, Mr Amory, and take a look for myself. Are there any casualties?'

'There are, I'm afraid, sir. Two men who went down to the messroom without orders.' Amory gave the names. 'The bodies were wedged behind a bulkhead that had curled itself around them. And the bosun. . . .'

'Tawney? Dead, d'you mean?'

Amory nodded. 'He went down to look at the damage and missed his footing – the broken plates had iced up already. One of the hands saw him go, nothing he could have done about it.' Amory saw the reaction in Theakston's face: the Old Man and Tawney had sailed together for many years, transferring together, at the request of each, to the various ships of the Bricker Dockett Line. Each had an enormous respect for the other and in the eyes of Captain Theakston, Tawney would have no replacement as bosun – this, Amory knew. And currently, with the ship in trouble, Jock Tawney and the two other seamen were going to be very badly missed. Amory said, 'We shall be short-handed now, sir. I was wondering if the Navy could assist. The PO, Napper – '

'To take Tawney's place? That'll be the day!' Theakston had already summed Napper up, but he shrugged and approached Kemp with Amory's request.

'Of course,' Kemp said. 'The ship comes before the guns now.' He turned to Cutler. 'Sub, send down to Napper. He's to give the chief officer any assistance needed – leave one gunnery rate to report to the bridge and man one of the Oerlikons until further orders. And the guard to remain on von Hagen's quarters, of course.'

'Aye, aye, sir.' Cutler turned away and went at the double down the starboard ladder. Kemp, hunched into his bridge coat and duffel coat, with the hood of the latter pulled over his uniform cap, stared down towards the shattered fo'c'sle. In the loom of light from the streamers in the sky he could pick out the jag of the lower bow plating, blown out at almost ninety degrees from the hull, although the deck plating of the fo'c'sle, together with the anchors and slips and the cables themselves, was intact. The collision bulkhead, set abaft the stem at the regulation five per cent of the ship's length, would have a colossal weight of water to hold if much speed was maintained. That bulkhead had specially thickened plating to withstand free water, and extra-strong stiffeners, but the thrust of water from the ship's head-way into wind and sea was a different kettle of fish and Theakston, when he had made his inspection, might want to reduce still further. Kemp did sums in his head: there would be a considerable delay in his arrival at Archangel and now he would have no hope whatsoever of catching up the convoy. He must proceed alone and unescorted through the Barents Sea and chance the attention of the heavy German ships coming down from the north to run into the inadequate guns of the escort under Rear-Admiral Fellowes. In the meantime there was nothing that he, personally, could do. Such was the lot of the Commodore of any convoy for much of the time. Just wait and hope and curb an abounding impatience. Inaction chafed at Kemp: it always had. But it was one of the limitations and frustrations of command at sea and along with the loneliness had to be accepted without complaint. Always the Captain was the loneliest man in the ship: in the RN the Captain lived alone and entered the friendliness of the wardroom only by invitation. In cargo ships as opposed to the liners, the master normally took his meals at the head of the table in the officers' saloon, but he was expected to leave them in peace afterwards and return to his own quarters and his own company. No one liked the master breathing down his neck.

Kemp brooded, his head sunk now on his arms crossed on the teak rail of the bridge. The loss of the *Portree* so suddenly had shaken him; the inability to pick up survivors was a sword-thrust. Neither event was Kemp's first experience of war by a long chalk but somehow this had been more personal: he had made the decision to reject the German demands and however correct and inevitable that decision had been he couldn't escape the knowledge that his order had led to the deaths of an entire ship's company. Fathers, husbands, sons – around one hundred and sixty of them, gone down beneath the freezing cold of the Barents Sea, leaving grief and despair to strike hard in many parts of the British Isles. Kemp thought of his own two sons, both of them at sea with the RN ... at any moment he too could be hit by bad news, he and Mary, the result of some other responsible senior officer's decision.

Kemp turned as he heard a step on the ladder: Theakston was coming back to the bridge. 'Well, Captain?'

'Not so good. The bulkhead's showing signs of strain. You know the principles, of course. The bulkheads bring total rigidity to their sections, making them unduly strong. The local excess must be distributed by the brackets to the stringers, shell plating and so on – '

'And the collision bulkhead more so – yes.'

Theakston said, 'My chief engineer and carpenter have had a look. They're not happy. Something's been set out of true by the impact of the explosion, you see.'

'The shoring beams'll help?'

Theakston nodded. 'Yes, to some extent. But not to be relied on if – '

'You want to reduce speed, is that it?'

'Yes. We have to, if we're to have any real hope. There's no alternative. Indeed I'd go further: in my opinion we should make sternway at least until Amory has the beams in position and chocked down. That way, we'll take all the strain off.'

'Damn slow progress!'

'Aye, it will be. But there's nowt else . . . and it's better than foundering.'

Kemp lifted his hands and let them fall again. 'Your ship, Captain. You have the right to save her.'

'Aye, and the duty too. I shall proceed astern. I shall review the position when Mr Amory reports the beams in place.' Theakston moved into the wheelhouse and gave his orders. The ship's head swung as the quartermaster brought her round on to a reciprocal of her course, and she rolled heavily as she came across the waves, then steadied as the swing was met by opposite helm and the engine-room telegraph was put to half astern. Theakston moved out once again to the wing, looking aft to see the water swirl for'ard as the sternway came on.

Kemp said, 'As I remarked – slow progress. How about putting her on full, Captain?'

'There'll be a deal of yaw.'

'I know it's not easy to keep on course astern. But there happens to be a need now.' Kemp's voice was sharper than he had intended.

'Oh, aye,' Theakston said. 'There's no call for anger.' He waited for a moment; Kemp, restraining his temper, said nothing. Theakston gave him a long stare and then marched away, back to the wheelhouse. Kemp heard the ring of the telegraph, followed by the repetition from below, and then the *Hardraw Falls* began to shudder to the full stern-thrust of her engines. Kemp let out a long breath: Yorkshiremen, he told himself firmly, had sterling virtues. . . .

ii

Amory had the hands hard at it, his own crew and the naval ratings. The shoring beams had been brought out and mostly set in place against the collision bulkhead, all ready to be wedged down with the chocks and blows of the carpenter's sledgehammer. Amory was in an impatient mood: Petty Officer Napper was as much use as a flea at a bullfight and managed to get constantly under everyone's feet at the wrong moment.

'Never set up shoring beams before, have you?' Amory asked.

'No, sir, I haven't,' Napper answered in an aggrieved tone that suggested that RN ships never got themselves into a situation where they needed to shore up, an attitude that infuriated Amory by its sheer nonsense. Napper was all thumbs and a loud voice, but fortunately the junior ratings had him weighed off and weren't taking too much notice of him, following the chief officer's orders instead. Napper didn't like that, and was fizzing like a fuse. He went on, 'Anyway, we do things different in the Andrew, see.' He added in a pained voice, 'That apart, sir, I've me injury. It don't help.'

'I don't suppose it does,' Amory said unsympathetically. 'Perhaps you'd rather go away and nurse it better.' He turned his back on Napper and lent a hand himself in the hefting of the final shoring beam into its place against the collision bulkhead, noting as he did so a small trickle of water forming a pool at the bottom of the bulkhead: not very serious so far but it might mean they wouldn't be able to resume moving with headway. Even if the bulkhead was only very slightly sprung Theakston couldn't risk bringing heavy pressure to bear. And then God alone knew how long it would take them to reach Archangel.

iii

Napper's ears had burned red: *nurse it better!* Who did Mr bloody Amory think he was? Regarding the chief officer's words as a dismissal, Napper took himself off in a huff, glad enough to get to hell away from the collision bulkhead, the vicinity of which was a potentially dangerous place. If the bulkhead should go suddenly, it would be all up with the hands nearby – they'd be engulfed, not just by water but by flung beams and breaking timber as well. Napper climbed ladders aft of the collision bulkhead and emerged from the starboard door beneath the fo'c'sle, coming into the fore well-deck and leaving the wreckage of the seaman's quarters behind him. He spared a fleeting thought for the deck-hands, now with most of their gear gone for a burton and their living quarters with it. From now on they would have to doss down where they could; it wouldn't be comfortable in

123

the alleyways and storerooms. Napper moved on. They had day-light in the sky now, dim and murky, and he saw Commodore Kemp looking down from the bridge, and at once he smartened his bearing so as to look as though he was going about his duties, and marched left-right-left while keeping a hand on the lifelines until he disappeared from view into the midship superstructure feeling like a moving icicle, even his lips cracking with frozen spittle. It came to him suddenly that he'd been talking to himself all the way up from the depths of the ship, first sign of madness, or in his case just a furious reaction to what Amory had said. Not that he hadn't enough to drive him crazy, what with Able Seaman Grove's cheek, and the perishing cold, and the bloody awful danger of being half disabled in the Barents Sea of all places, and the fact that he should have been sitting comfy in Pompey barracks drinking a cup of char while the matloes car-ried out part-of-ship duties around the parade and blocks.

On his way to the chief steward's office for another look at *The Ship Captain's Medical Guide* Napper passed the foot of the ladder leading up to the officers' accommodation and became aware that his name was being called.

He halted and looked up: the armed seaman who was sup-posed to be guarding the Nazi's cabin was at the head of the ladder. 'PO?'

'Yer. What are you doing, deserting your place of duty, lad? Bloody Jerry could break out, couldn't he? And then what, I'd like to know!'

'Sorry, PO. It's the prisoner.'

'What about him?'

'Says he's ill.'

'Ha! Ill, is he?' Napper lifted his cap and scratched at his thin-ning hair. 'What's he got?' he asked hoarsely, his own interest in medical matters coming to the fore.

'I dunno, just ill.'

'Hang on.' Napper climbed the ladder and accompanied the sentry back to von Hagen's cabin door. He thumped on it. 'Petty Officer o' the Guard here,' he said in a loud voice. 'What's the trouble, eh?'

There was no answer. Once again Napper scratched at his head, pondering. What was the Jerry playing at? Could be dead for all Napper knew, or could be dying, and if he was allowed to

124

die then somebody would be sure to blame Napper for losing a valuable source of information. On the other hand, Napper was buggered if he was going to open up the cabin door, notwithstanding the sentry's rifle and bayonet. Nazis were slippery customers and up to all manner of tricks, like monkeys. 'Hang on,' Napper said once more, and went fast for the bridge to report to the Commodore.

Kemp asked, 'How genuine do you think this is?'

'No idea, sir. The prisoner, 'e didn't utter after I got there, sir.'

Kemp looked at Cutler. He said, 'Something I didn't think about but should have. Agents ... they're said to be supplied with lethal tablets, keep 'em in their mouths or something ready to swallow.'

'I doubt if it's that, sir. He'd have taken it back in Norway, when he was nabbed. Or aboard the submarine.'

Kemp grunted. 'Yes, perhaps.'

Napper said, 'If it had been that, sir, he wouldn't have said he was ill.'

'That's right,' Cutler agreed. 'They act fast. Instantaneously.'

Kemp said, 'We'll have to investigate. I'll go down myself. You'll stand by with the sentry, Napper.'

'Yessir.'

Kemp went along the ladder, followed by Cutler and Napper. He approached the cabin door and knocked on it. 'Kemp here. What's the trouble, von Hagen?'

Again there was no response; Kemp banged again, with no result. He stood back, and nodded at the sentry. 'Right,' he said. 'Aim for the doorway. I'm going to open up. Hand me the key. If there's any trouble, shoot – but not to kill him. Just to disable.'

'Aye, aye, sir.' The sentry passed the key to Kemp, who put it in the lock and turned it. As he did so he felt pressure on the door and started to call a warning to the others. Before the words were out of his mouth the door came open with a crash, sending Kemp flat on his back as von Hagen emerged like a bullet, fists flailing. The sentry fired and missed, just before he too was bowled over, and the bullet singed past the German into the cabin. A fist connected with Napper's jaw and he lurched back against a bulkhead as von Hagen ran along the alleyway for the door at the end, the door to the open deck running alongside the officers' cabins. Kemp was up and in pursuit as fast as he could make it; he and the sentry went through the door to find von Hagen climbing the guardrail. Below, the cold sea rose and fell as the ship rolled. Kemp reached the guardrail, calling out to von Hagen, got a grip on the German as he jumped and was himself lifted to the rail. Before he could let go his grip, he had lost his balance and was plummeting with von Hagen towards the sea's freezing cold. The sentry reached the rail and reacted fast.

'Man overboard starboard!' He yelled the words up towards the bridge and at the same time grabbed a lifebuoy from its stowage on the rail and threw it, with its securing line running out behind it, towards the heads visible in the water close by the ship's side.

As the lifebuoy took the water, the sound of aircraft engines was heard coming in from the direction of the Kola Inlet.

THIRTEEN

Theakston was leaning out over the water from the bridge wing, his face angry. 'Damned idiot! Why didn't he let the German go, for God's sake?' He had stopped engines and was about to order a boat to be lowered from the falls when the sound of the aircraft engines came and he left the open bridge and doubled into the wheelhouse to press the action alarm. Strident din echoed through the ship. For'ard at the collision bulkhead Amory ordered the naval gunnery rates to their close-range weapons, remained himself with half a dozen of the crew to tend the beams. Any fresh strain coming on the bulkhead could mean total disaster unless men were handy for instant response, not that they would be able to do a lot if the shoring beams themselves should crumple.

On the deck outside the officers' accommodation, Petty Officer Napper was in a state of dither: should he lend a hand with rescuing the Commodore or should he get to his action station pronto? 'Christ,' he said to no one in particular, 'this bloody would go and happen!'

It was Cutler who solved his problem. 'Bugger off, Napper, and get shooting – I've got the line and the fish is on the hook.' He'd seen Kemp reach out and grasp the lifebuoy, pull it in to his body so that he could take a turn of the line itself around his waist. Kemp's other hand was fast on von Hagen's collar. So far, so good, Cutler thought. They could both be hauled aboard just as long as Kemp's frozen fingers could retain his grip on the German. If they couldn't – too bad; at least Kemp had the line fast, and now a heavier line was going down to him. It was a question of speed, of getting them out from the water and into the warm. The Commodore was no longer young and the submersion could be enough to finish him off. As Cutler hauled in, assisted by the sentry, there was a rattle of gunfire above his head and bullets spattered the gray-painted bulkhead behind him.

ii

'Fighters,' Theakston said as he ducked down behind the bridge screen. A line of bullet holes dotted the deck planks and panes of glass shattered in the wheelhouse. From monkey's island above, the Bofors and Lewis guns cracked out, a sustained return of fire towards the belly of a German fighter, which missed its mark. Petty Officer Napper, feeling dangerously exposed so high up in the ship, his stomach loosening fast, saw the bigger shapes of JU 88 bombers: the Nazis had evidently been carrying out an attack on the Russian military and naval installations in the Kola Inlet, probably concentrating on Murmansk where, for all Napper knew, a homeward convoy could be assembling. Deciding that the ship's master might like to know his prognostications, Napper made a dive for the vertical ladder down to the bridge as two more fighters came in from the south. And just in time, he reckoned a moment later as the fighters came in again and cannon fire swept monkey's island and there was a scream of agony from one of the gunnery rates. Another second's delay and he would have caught that lot up. Napper had felt his bravery seeping away with every knot made, this trip. . . .

He approached Captain Theakston in the lull that followed. Theakston said, 'No bombing. I wonder if they've been warned about the German aboard us.'

'Maybe, sir. Maybe it's just that they've already dropped their load on Murmansk. If that's the case –'

'We can consider ourselves lucky! They may not bother overmuch with us, if they're bound back to base.'

'Well, sir, I dunno.' Napper wiped the back of his glove across his face. He wanted to keep Theakston talking; if he remained with him, the wheelhouse was handy to dodge into when the next attack came. 'They'll be bound south for Norway, see. That means they deviated out, special like, when they picked us up.'

128

'We shall have to see,' Theakston said. He turned as Cutler came up the ladder, his duffel coat stiff with frozen seawater. 'Well, lad?'

'Both aboard, sir.' Cutler was breathing heavily. 'Being stripped and given brandy by the chief steward. Blankets, hot-water bottles. I don't think they're too bad, considering. Commodore wanted to come to the bridge.' Cutler grinned. 'Afraid I took your name in vain, sir. Said you'd have him removed by force – your personal order.'

Theakston gave a thin smile, about the first time Cutler had seen his face relax. 'He took it?'

'Like a lamb.'

'That doesn't speak too well for how he's feeling, does it?'

Cutler said, 'As a matter of fact, he did try to come up. But his legs gave away. I still don't think he's too bad, sir, all the same.'

Theakston nodded; he wished Kemp well but was not displeased to have his own bridge to himself for as long as it took Kemp to recover. Cutler looked at Napper, hovering by the wheelhouse door. 'Everything under control?' he asked.

'Yessir. Casualties on monkey's island, but – '

'And you, Petty Officer Napper?'

Napper stared and felt uncomfortable. 'Me, sir?'

'Yes, you. What precisely are you doing?'

Napper said, 'Advising the Captain, sir. About the aircraft, sir. I said like, they've been giving Murmansk a pasting – ' He broke off as two more fighters came in, keeping low, appearing suddenly from the murk to rake the decks once again. The noise was deafening as everything opened on them: their cannon fire ricocheted from bulkheads and stanchions, peppered the funnel and the funnel casings, slammed into the griped-in lifeboats at the falls, and left pock-marks along the length of the boat deck. From above the engineers' accommodation aft the close-range crews pumped out bullets, firing almost vertically as the aircraft roared across, lying back in the straps to increase the angle as far as possible, but the fighters passed on unhit, vanishing as suddenly as they had appeared.

'They'll be back,' Cutler said edgily. Air attack was a bloody business and, Cutler thought, no one ever got used to it. Probably it grew worse the longer you were subjected to it. It brought him a feeling of total helplessness: ack-ack fire, he believed, was no more than a gesture, to shoot down aircraft was easier said than done unless you were part of a big fleet with a huge flak umbrella. They came in suddenly, at high speed, raked you or bombed you, and were gone before you could lay or train with any effect. But as it turned out, they didn't come back this time. When more aircraft sounds were heard they were from the north; and it was Napper who identified them first.

'Ours, sir . . . Fleet Air Arm! Seafires, sir!'

Seafires, the naval version of the Spitfire, were fast and furious. No wonder the Nazis hadn't lingered. Cutler, looking up through his binoculars, said, 'Carrier from the Home Fleet. Thank God!' A cheer went up raggedly from the decks as the Seafires were recognized and as one of them detached from the squadron to circle the *Hardraw Falls* a lamp was seen to be winking from it. Leading Signalman Corrigan read off the message and reported to Cutler. 'Signal, sir: "Message intercepted from Murmansk indicates heavy damage to port installations. Fairway blocked by sunken vessels awaiting QP convoy homeward. Do not attempt to enter." Message ends, sir.'

Theakston lifted an eyebrow. 'That pilot's making assumptions, I reckon, all about nowt. We're still bound for Archangel far as I know.'

'He's seen our damage, sir,' Cutler said. 'He thinks we'll alter – ' He broke off. 'Signalling again, Corrigan.'

'Yes, sir. "Do you require assistance."'

Cutler looked interrogatively at Theakston, who said, 'That's for the Commodore, lad. Best ask him.'

'I'll go down,' Cutler said. He slid down the ladder, the palms of his gloved hands sliding on the rails thick with ice. He knocked at Kemp's door and went in on the heels of the knock. Kemp, blue in the face and shivering, managed to give him a grin.

'All right, sir?'

'Oh, I'll survive, never fear! What's the state of things, Sub?'

Cutler reported. He added, 'Seafires from the Home Fleet, sir. Ask, do we require assistance.'

At first Kemp made no comment, giving an oblique response. 'Those Seafires . . . any indication of contact between the Home Fleet and the Germans?'

'No, sir – '

'Ask them, then. Keep me informed – then I'll make a final decision about assistance. I'll probably enter Murmansk and to hell with the orders about von Hagen.'

Cutler shook his head. 'No hope of that, sir.' He reported the blocked fairway as a result of heavy attack. 'It'll have to be Archangel, sir. If anywhere at all.'

'You sound defeatist,' Kemp said sharply. 'Don't. Now – up top and contact the Seafires.'

Cutler went back to the bridge at the rush. Corrigan passed the Commodore's message: the answer came back that up to the time the Seafires had been flown off from their parent carrier there had been no contact but the C-in-C was steaming to stand between the PQ convoy and the threat from the north. Cutler sent an acknowledgment and went down again to report to the Commodore.

Kemp said, 'I'm going to take a chance that C-in-C Home Fleet'll reinforce the escort – or order 'em to rejoin the convoy if they've moved north to engage the enemy as we guessed they might. And now the Home Fleet's here, it's only prudent to accept the offer of assistance. Make a signal to the aircraft, Cutler – my thanks and I'd appreciate a destroyer or corvette to stand by me. All right?'

'Yes, sir, Commodore.' Cutler returned to the bridge at the double and the message was passed. A few minutes later the Seafire banked and turned away. The gunners were fallen out from action stations and reduced to two watches once again. Petty Officer Napper went round the gun positions and saw to the removal of two bodies from monkey's island. Going aft he found Able Seaman Grove flinging his arms about his body, his teeth chattering.

'Got away with it again, did you?' Napper asked in a surly tone.

Grove grinned, cheeky as ever, Napper thought. 'That's a nicely expressed sentiment from a bloke's PO, I *don't* think.'

'Get stuffed,' Napper said.

iii

The cold seemed to increase, although it hadn't seemed possible that it could worsen. The temperature stood at nearly fifty degrees below freezing. The *Hardraw Falls* made desperately slow progress in her sternway motion; the collision bulkhead, watched constantly by Amory and the ship's acting bosun and the carpenter, was holding yet and the seepage hadn't got any worse, though this was probably due to the lack of water pressure even though some water was splashing up against the bulkhead as a bitter east wind drove against the metal. By nightfall Kemp was back on the bridge, his sea-soaked bridge coat and duffel coat dried out in the galley. He still looked a little pinched about the mouth but otherwise, he insisted, was fit enough, and he didn't like being confined to his cabin. Von Hagen, according to the chief steward, was also recovering but was in a state of serious depression. Kemp said he would talk to the German agent in the morning: he preferred to let him stew for the time being. If the depressive state worsened, he might be made to be more forthcoming: Kemp still had in mind his orders to extract any information that was going.

At a little before midnight the snow started again, coming down heavily and at times almost horizontally, borne along that piercing east wind that felt as though it was coming direct from the Siberian wastes. Emerging from the comparative warmth of the ship's interior into the driving snow was sheer torture. Cutler, staying on the bridge with the Commodore, was concerned for Kemp. In his view, Kemp didn't look at all fit. Cutler came out with it straight, said he ought to go below. There was nothing he could do by remaining in an exposed position: with the shattered glass of the screens, there was no protection even in the wheelhouse although temporary canvas dodgers had been secured across the lower halves.

'I'm all right, Cutler.'

'You won't be by the morning, sir.'

Kemp said, 'Do you know something, Cutler? I served my time, my apprenticeship, in sail. I just caught up the tail end of the windjammer era. Four years, a little more by the time I had my second mate's ticket, then three more for first mate and master. I was on the South American and Australian run ... around Cape Horn for Chilean ports – Puerrto Montt, Valparaiso, Iquique, and then across to Sydney, Melbourne, Adelaide, Fremantle. Cape Horn, the Australian Bight – the Horn especially, of course – the Barents Sea has nothing on them.'

'You were younger then, sir.'

Kemp laughed. 'Kindly don't remind me! You're right, of course, but we were given a toughness that lasted. I'll remain on the bridge, Cutler. Don't forget that damaged bow. And don't forget that in this muck, we're going to be hard to find.'

'You mean the ship detatched from the escort to stand by us, sir?'

'Exactly. I want to be handy. There's no need for you to stay. You've done your share, Cutler. Go below and get some sleep – and that's an order.'

After Cutler had left the bridge Kemp wedged himself into a corner of the bridge wing and sunk his head down on to his arms crossed on the guardrail, the hood of his duffel coat pulled down over his ears. He faced aft, in the direction of the ship's sternway, into the appalling drive of the heavy snow. The night was very dark now, no sight of the Northern Lights, with only the faint loom that was always present over the world's oceans to allow a faint glimpse of the snowflakes. The ship was covered now, its outline vanishing more positively than in the earlier blizzard. Kemp's thoughts, once aroused by his brief conversation with Cutler, went back to those early days at sea.

Happy times, however hard – good comradeship and the world at his feet as the wind blew a sixteen-year-old youth in his old windjammer away from Liverpool town on a thirty-thousand-mile round journey. A motley enough crew at times, but all of them knowing that each depended on the other for his life in the many dangerous situations that could and did arise. Kemp recalled the desperate battering into the teeth of the westerlies off the pitch of the Horn – Cape Stiff, as the old shellbacks had known it – the attempts to find a shift of that neverending wind that would carry them round towards the South Pacific. On many a voyage a ship had taken up to six long weeks of cold and hunger to beat round, with all hands and the cook aloft on the swaying footropes to take in sail or adjust the trim, frozen hands grabbing at frozen canvas whipping in the gale and sometimes throwing men off the yards to land on deck with broken backs or go sheer into the icy water with no hope of rescue. One hand for the ship and one for yourself had been the watchword, but with some of the more bullying mates right behind you, you didn't take that too literally : the discipline was iron hard, even at times sadistic, and if you didn't survive, you didn't and that was that. No questions asked afterwards, no letters of complaint to Members of Parliament. 'Lost overboard' was the notation in the log, and that was enough.

Why had he ever gone to sea ? Why had he endured the hardships, the food that consisted of such messes as burgoo, cracker hash, sea pie, weevily biscuits, corned dog and so on, why had he settled for no pay as an apprentice and the gradual advancement to what was then a master's niggardly twelve pounds a month ?

He grinned to himself: it had been bred into him by his old grandmother . . . her father had been a master in sail and so had Kemp's grandfather, her husband ; their memories had been idolized and kept alive in the young Kemp's home, and he had listened to many yarns of the old times and had become imbued with a perhaps over-romanticized view of the seafaring life, a life of adventure far removed from the humdrum business of the shore. Seamen were a race apart, with a different set of values of honesty and fair dealing, men working together for the good of each and for the ship ; ships had been prideful things to sailors and to Kemp's grandmother. He had found the reality not quite the same as the dream but even so there was still some of the romance left, some of it in the form of the shantymen and the nostalgic songs sung with the fiddler on the capstan as a ship put out to sea for a voyage that could last two years before they sighted a home port again. Stirring times for a young man, experiences that had left behind them that enduring physical hardness of which he had just spoken to Cutler. But Cutler would probably never really understand, even though he clearly liked the sea himself, even though his own country of America had also had a long sea tradition of hard men and hard-driven ships, bucko mates in plenty and grim masters who pounded the down-easters along the trade routes of the world, ruling their kingdoms with the fist and the belaying-pin, and the cruel punishments of being mastheaded for long periods in bitter weather or in blazing tropic sun.

Kemp gave a sudden deep-seated shiver: the immersion hadn't in fact done him any good and never mind the hardness of sail. As Cutler had hinted, he was growing old – at any rate in

Cutler's eyes. In his own view, the early fifties didn't make anyone an old man. Kemp shook himself free of the snow that covered him, and beat his arms around his body. Old be buggered!

iv

The *Hardraw Falls*, missing bosun Tawney, was by now short of officers as well: a watch had to be kept at the collision bulkhead as well as on the bridge, which meant the Captain had to take a turn on his own. The bridge watch was being split between Theakston and the second officer, while Amory and the third officer shared the duty for'ard, protected from the weather but as bitterly cold, or almost, as the bridge. There was a deadness, a particular kind of coldness, about being enclosed in metal that you couldn't touch with an unprotected fingertip unless you wanted the flesh to freeze to what was touched and remain there until it was torn bloodily away. Amory, taking the middle watch, the twelve to four known at sea as the graveyard watch, walked up and down with difficulty, dodging past the great beams that shored up the collision bulkhead, for'ard of Number One hold with its lethal cargo of high explosive, trying to keep his circulation going. For want of anything better to think about as he kept an eye lifting for trouble, Amory, like Kemp, found his mind going back into the past, fruitlessly and painfully. The bomb that had killed Felicity had changed Amory a good deal and he had little left in life except a consuming hatred for the Nazis. The killing of Nazis was his interest now; he wanted to live so that he could go on contributing what he could to the defeat of Hitler's pestilential doctrines, so that he could have the final satisfaction of seeing the Allied armies entering Berlin, even though he would see it only on the newsreels in his local cinema – that, and the surrender of the German Navy, the last striking of their detested, flaunted ensign.

Vengeful?

Amory gave a hard, humourless laugh. Of course it was, and why not? He'd had the prospect of a whole life to live with Felicity; now all he had to go home to was a crusty and widowed father, pensioned off, too old now even for the police War Reserve, and not liking it, and taking it out on his neighbours as an air-raid warden. On leave, Amory had heard him at it: *'Put that light out ... don't you know there's a war on ... who the hell d'you think you are?'* He'd also heard the remarks, sotto voce when he was recognized, in the local pub, about the old bastard who thought he was still a police super.

Not much of a life, on leave. Might just as well stay aboard the ship, really. Better, in fact: Amory was a vigorous man with normal wants. The girls were more co-operative in the seaports than at home with their little respectabilities and what would the neighbours think. Amory meant girls – not prostitutes. He'd been at sea quite long enough to see the results of risks taken in extremity. For the same reason he was always careful not to drink too much: tight, you lost your discrimination and the urge grew stronger even if the ability tended to lessen at the crucial moment. . . .

Up and down, up and down, half stumbling with sheer tiredness, frozen right through, the very marrow in the bones feeling it. The ship heaving, groaning, weird and disquieting noises from distorted frames. Could they ever reach Archangel, arse first, at little more than four knots?

Just watch the bulkhead, that was the thing. Forget the past, don't worry about the future – just watch the bulkhead for the smallest sign of further strain. Amory knew that if anything happened it was likely to happen suddenly and he wouldn't have much time to clear the compartment.

v

Dawn came, weak and straggly, no sun but still the everlasting blizzard. It was no more than a faint lifting of the dark, you couldn't really call it a dawn. Kemp had at last given in and gone below when Theakston had come up at 0400 hours to take over the bridge from the second officer. Once on his bunk, he had dropped off to sleep almost fully dressed – weariness had overcome him by the time he'd got his outer clothing and seaboots off. At 0800 his steward, Torrence, looked in, shook his head at the inert figure and went out again, closing the door gently behind him. Moving along the alleyway he met Cutler. 'Good morning, sir,' he said briskly. 'Not that it is.'

'Morning, Torrence. How's the Commodore?'

'Sleeping, sir, flat out and snoring. I was going to bring 'is breakfast but I thought, well, why disturb 'im, sir, let 'im rest.' Torrence flicked at a speck on his white jacket. 'Did you want 'im, like?'

Cutler shook his head. 'No. But he wanted to see the prisoner . . . leave him for now, though. Keep a watch now and again, all right? And let me know when he's awake.'

'I'll watch over 'im like a mother, sir,' Torrence said cheerfully. Cutler was glad of the happy tone; there had been too many long faces around the last few days. Not surprising since there was nothing to be cheerful about, but depressing.

Even more depressing was the snow, which was cutting them off from all contact with the outside world; he felt they were like a blind man trying to walk across Dartmoor. They moved in a world of their own with no knowing if the promised destroyer or corvette from the escort would ever reach them.

Cutler went back to the bridge, refreshed after what passed in wartime for a full night's sleep. He had just reached the wheel-house when there was a buzz from the wireless room and Theakston, who was handing over the watch once again to the second officer, answered it. He swung round on Cutler.

'Signal from the Admiralty,' he said. 'In cypher. Prefixed Most Immediate.'

FOURTEEN

Cutler brought out his naval decyphering tables and broke down the signal into plain language. Then, need for sleep or not, he knew he had to call the Commodore.

Kemp came awake at once, the attribute of a seaman, the ability to clear the mind fast.

'What is it, Cutler?'

'Signal from the Admiralty, sir.' Cutler held out the naval message form and Kemp read fast, his forehead creased into a frown.

'God damn and blast,' he said. 'What do the buggers expect of us?'

'Miracles, sir?'

'It bloody well looks like it!' Kemp swung his legs off the bunk and stood up. He swayed a little and reached out to steady himself on the bunk board, reading the signal again as if he hadn't taken it in fully the first time. It read: 'Moscow anxious about delay. Vital repeat vital that passenger reaches Archangel within seventy-two hours of time of origin of this signal. Met reports now indicate freeze likely at any time.'

Kemp said, 'So we take orders from the Kremlin now.'

'Seems so, sir.' Cutler paused. 'Why not have breakfast, then – '

'Oh, balls to breakfast, Cutler. I told you I was tough. We didn't often have *breakfast* in the windjammers in the old days!'

Cutler grinned. 'The days when ships were wood, and men were made of iron?'

Kemp stopped in the act of pulling on his monkey-jacket and stared at his assistant. 'Where the hell did *you* hear that?'

'Read it somewhere, sir.'

'You surprise me, Cutler. But never mind. I'll be on the bridge directly. I'll take a look at the chart on the way.'

'Aye, aye, sir – '

'And my compliments to the Captain . . . tell him what's in the signal and say I'll be asking for the impossible – more speed.'

'Yes, sir.' Cutler left the cabin and went back to the bridge. Theakston had in fact gone below. After a word with the second officer Cutler used the voice-pipe to the master's quarters and gave him the news. There was a curse but Theakston was back on the bridge before Kemp had entered the chartroom.

Theakston said, 'I can't get any more out of her, lad, and that's flat.'

'Perhaps a knot or two, sir?'

'Just you say that to my chief engineer! Engines don't like going astern for too long. Or too fast. She has to be nursed. And there's another point, isn't there?'

'What's that, sir?'

'The visibility. Just look at it, eh?'

Cutler nodded: the snow was thickening and the visibility was down to something like two cables, coming down farther in patches as an extra swirl of snow was driven into their faces. 'Bad,' he said. 'But I doubt if there's much shipping around.'

'Oh, no! Only maybe a homeward convoy coming the other way.' Theakston lifted his binoculars and stared into the white blanket ahead; then lowered them again. It wasn't worth the effort of lifting, the glasses brought up only a thicker blank. He said no more; a couple of minutes later Kemp emerged from the chartroom and approached Theakston.

'Good morning, Captain. You'll have heard about the signal . . . I've just looked at the last dead reckoning position on the chart. We have around four hundred miles to go. Say a hundred hours' steaming . . . it's too much, in the light of that signal.'

'There's nowt to be done about it, Commodore.' Theakston's tone was stubborn; Kemp had expected no less. He pressed, but tactfully. The ship was Theakston's responsibility, he reminded himself for the hundredth time since leaving the Firth of Lorne. Theakston, however, did come under the overall orders of the Trade Division of the Admiralty as he did himself, and if necessary, with reluctance, Kemp would make the point forcefully.

Theakston said, 'She'll not take more speed ... just maybe another knot,' he added grudgingly as he saw the set of Kemp's jaw.

'I shall need more than that, Captain. I'm sorry, but there it is. We have the Kremlin at our throats, if that's not too dramatic a ·phrase – '

'I give nowt for the Kremlin.'

Kemp laughed. 'I don't give much myself. But I do have my orders. And there's the ice – we haven't all that long. The signal says it's vital – you know the contents.'

'Aye, I do. Why is it so vital?'

'I don't know. I'm just the Commodore.'

'You should maybe find out from the prisoner.'

'That,' Kemp said, 'is what I propose to do – to try to, anyway. But in the meantime we can't afford to fall behind the progress of the freeze off Archangel. I have to assume the Admiralty knows its own business.'

Theakston's face was aggresive. 'I said, there's nowt – '

'Yes, I know. I'm going for'ard, Captain – '

'What for?'

Kemp said, 'To look at the collision bulkhead.' He didn't wait for any explosion from Theakston; he turned away and went down the starboard ladder to the well-deck, into the fo'c'sle accommodation and down again to where Amory was once again at his station abaft the bulkhead, watching the shoring beams.

ii

The word had spread quickly that something extra was in the wind along with the blinding snow, that fresh orders had reached the Commodore. No one knew what it was, but all were certain it wasn't good news: it never was, in wartime. Chief Steward Buckle nabbed Petty Officer Napper as the latter went crab-wise past his office.

'Mr Napper – '

'Yer?'

'No better, eh?'

'Worse.'

'Well, well. Never mind, it'll clear up soon, bound to.' Buckle lowered his voice. 'Heard the buzz, I s'pose?'

'Yer. What about it? You heard something too?'

'Not me – Torrence, Captain's steward. Flapping ears. He says it's to do with the Russians. Well, of course, I know we're bound for Russia, so I reckon there may not be anything special in it, but then again, you never bloody well know, do you?'

'Not often, no. Brassbound buggers don't give much away to the lower deck, not usually.' Napper sucked at his teeth, glad to have someone of about his own status to moan to: and it wasn't often he got called mister, and he was flattered and grateful. 'Want to know what I reckon? It's that there Nazi, my prisoner.' Napper liked the sound of 'my prisoner' and said it again. 'If 'e wasn't my responsibility, I reckon I'd do 'im in and settle it. Another thing – I reckon Stalin comes into it somewhere.'

'Stalin, eh? How?'

Napper shrugged. 'I dunno. Just does. I don't like it, not at all I don't. I reckon we'll never be allowed to leave bloody Archangel ever again.'

'Go on!'

Napper wagged a finger. 'You just see. That Stalin and 'is secret police, OGPU, isn't it? I dunno the ins and outs like. But we're carrying a load o' dynamite and I don't mean the flipping cargo either. That there von whatsit, Hagen ... and Stalin, 'e won't be letting us off the hook once we're in 'is grasp. You mark my words, Mr Buckle. We're *political* now. Bloody *political*. You know what that means.'

Buckle didn't, but he nodded sagely. 'Dirty,' he said. 'Dirty bastards the lot of them, politicians.'

'Out for their own ends like, all the time. . . .'

It wasn't only Torrence who had flapping ears. So the word spread. The *Hardraw Falls* was to be seized by the Russians the moment she entered Archangel. But in the meantime there were other and more immediate worries. Napper was still talking to the chief steward when the ship gave a lurch and her roll increased sharply. There seemed to be a shift of wind at the same time, a curious silence on one side and a battering of waves on the other, and a sudden heightening of the creaks and groans that had started soon after the bow had been blown apart.

'Christ above,' Napper said in an alarmed tone, 'they're turn-

ing the bloody ship around! And I don't reckon it's back the way
we came either!'

Kemp was well aware of the enormous risk: but there was an
emergency and in his view the risk was justifiable in the new circumstances. Amory had reported the collision bulkhead holding
up; it should be capable of taking the strain so long as it didn't
go on for too long and so long as no attempt was made to go
beyond half speed. Theakston had been aghast at Kemp's sug-
gestion, but Kemp had been firm, as obstinate as Theakston himself, and in the end had quoted the Trade Division's authority.
Theakston had said he wanted it entered in the ship's official log
that he, as master, had objected strenuously but had been over-
ruled by the Commodore. He wanted it entered also that in his
view the ship would be in immediate danger of foundering with
all hands.

'I shall take full responsibility,' Kemp said.

'Aye, and that's to go in the log as well.'

'It will. It's very proper of you to insist, Captain – '

'Thank you for nowt!' Theakston snapped. 'I know my job as
master.'

Kemp hadn't liked it; he understood Theakston's point of
view very well, and would have had a similar reaction himself if
his command had been interfered with. But that signal had had
every possible ring of urgency; and reading between the lines
Kemp believed that the delivery of von Hagen had become more
important than the *Hardraw Falls* herself or her cargo, however
vital that might be, and was, to the Russian war effort and the
repulse of Hitler's hordes. On the other hand, to lose the ship
would be to lose von Hagen as well, a prospect that would
scarcely command itself to the Admiralty or the Russians. So it
was to be a calculated risk, everything depending now on the
collision bulkhead and its ability to withstand the pressures of
wind, snow and the Barents Sea.

When the ship made the turn, with Theakston clicking his
tongue at every shudder, Kemp went below to talk to von
Hagen. As on the previous occasions, he spoke to the German

alone, with the armed sentry standing by outside and backed up by Petty Officer Napper. Von Hagen, Kemp thought, looked a sick man: the immersion was still having its effect, and the Nazi's face was drawn and full of stress. He lay on his side on the bunk, fingers plucking.

Kemp asked, 'How are you feeling now, von Hagen?'

'Not good. But not all that bad.'

'I'm glad to hear that. It was a damn stupid thing to do – going overboard.'

Von Hagen laughed, a sad and bitter sound. 'And that, if I may say so, Captain Kemp, is a damn stupid thing to say! Isn't the Barents Sea better than Siberia – or any other kind of lingering death the Russians might inflict on me?'

Kemp shrugged. 'You have a point, I don't deny. But – '

'But you are going to do your best for me. You said that. I may not be handed over – you said.' The eyes gleamed in sardonic humour. 'Do you still say that?'

'I gave no promises of success. Only of trying . . . and that I shall do. I gave you my word on that.'

'Yes. I'm sorry.'

'But I still ask your help. I want to know many things, von Hagen.' Kemp had sat in the chair close to the bunk; now he leaned forward and spoke insistently. 'I want any information – you know this already – that you have in your head. Tell me that, and you will have a better chance. Oh, I know you believe a British Intelligence officer will board us, but you can't be sure of that, not wholly sure. And there's another and more specific thing I want to know.'

'And that is?'

Kemp said, 'What your personal importance is. I believe there's something beyond your acquired knowledge that makes it so vital that you be handed over to the Russians. Why should Britain agree to part with you? What's behind all this, von Hagen?'

'Call it the dirt of inter-governmental intrigue.'

'Yes. I know all that. But what's the reason?'

'It wouldn't help you, old friend! You would still have your duty to do . . . and if possible your promise to keep, your promise to try to help.'

'It's not a question of possibility or otherwise. That promise stands. But I'd like to be forearmed with the full story, the whys and wherefores. And I don't see that you would lose anything by telling me.'

Von Hagen shook his head and blew out his breath in something like despair. 'What makes you think I know?'

'Because you are an agent, and a top one as I understand it.'

'It makes no difference. In Germany, in the Third Reich, there are many secrets and they are strictly kept. There are so many right hands that don't know what the left ones are up to. In any case it is not my people, not the Government, who are handing me over, is it?'

'No. But I thought that with your special knowledge – '

'Yes, yes, I understand.'

'And I believe you do know, von Hagen.'

'Then you must continue to believe that. I cannot enlighten you. For the sake of an old friendship, I ask you not to press any further.' There was the glimmer of a smile. 'Like your former Prime Minister Stanley Baldwin on a certain occasion, my lips are sealed!'

iv

'I'm driven to the conclusion,' Kemp said to Cutler later, 'that the reason's personally discreditable to von Hagen and he doesn't want to talk about it.'

'Such as, maybe, he's operated inside Russia?'

'Possibly committed atrocities there.'

'Pure revenge on the part of the Russians, sir?'

Kemp nodded. 'One can't blame them. But I'm not sure I like being used as an agent of revenge. Especially as I've known the man so well.'

'Some years ago now, sir.'

Kemp raised his eyebrows. 'What the hell difference does that make?'

'Sorry, sir. But in fact there *is* a difference. Just the fact we've gone to war since then.'

'Don't try to teach me about loyalty, Cutler.'

'No, sir.' Cutler gave a cough and went off at a tangent. 'There's something you may have noticed. I certainly have.'

'What?'

'The crew, sir. Funny atmosphere. It's spread to the naval party too.'

'I hadn't noticed, no. Can you expand, Cutler?'

Cutler screwed up his face. 'Hard to pinpoint it, but there's a wary look and everyone's on edge over something – '

'Over von Hagen for my money! That's natural, if the galley wireless has painted word pictures about the man.'

'Sure, but I think it goes deeper. It's not the danger to the ship either. Or I don't think so. It's . . . oh, I guess I really don't know, sir . . . something about the voyage itself maybe. . . .'

'That's not very explicit, is it?' Kemp looked hard at the young sub-lieutenant's face: clearly Cutler was anxious and was disinclined to let the matter go by default. Kemp believed there was nothing in it; Cutler hadn't the sea experience to understand the gloom that so often affected a ship and her crew. On the liner run to Australia a miasma of ridiculous depression usually settled over the crew once they had left Fremantle homeward bound for the London River and Tilbury. It was a feeling that they simply couldn't wait to see the white cliffs of Dover again and another long voyage done. They called it an attack of the Channels. It was pretty well universal.

Cutler said, 'With your permission, sir, I'll have a word with Petty Officer Napper.'

'I wouldn't if I were you. All you'll get is a classified list of symptoms. But if you really want to, don't mind me!'

v

'I dunno, sir.'

'Oh, come off it, Napper. *Petty Officer* Napper. I thought Navy senior rates kept a finger on the pulse.'

'Well, yes, sir, they does, that's true.' Petty Officer Napper, who believed that it could have been his conversation with Buckle that had started the buzz about dangers waiting in Archangel on its rounds, was trying to be non-committal. 'I remember once, sir, when I was in the old *Emperor of India*, the commander – '

'Okay. Project your mind into the here and now, all right?'

Daft little bugger, Napper thought angrily, still wet behind the ears was Cutler. In an aggrieved tone he said, 'The hands is worried, that I've noticed, yes. They don't like going into Russian waters, sir. No more do I.'

'For God's sake . . . they aren't cannibals!'

'Not far off, sir. Not far off.'

'Oh, boloney – '

'Tisn't, sir! I've 'eard yarns, seen it in the papers, spitting babies on bayonets and frying the poor little sods like eggs – '

'That was the Nazis.'

'Oh.'

'Or said to be. And I don't know about the frying, that's a new one. Back to the point, Petty Officer Napper: what's the mood?'

'They're pissed off, sir.'

'That all? They'll get over it.'

Napper was just about to say, but had decided not to in case he got any backlash, that the mood was nasty and deteriorating, when there was a sudden booming sound from for'ard and the *Hardraw Falls* checked her way through the water as the engines shuddered to full astern.

FIFTEEN

Theakston reacted fast: the moment he heard that hollow booming sound he had personally wrenched the telegraph over to emergency full astern. In the engine-room Chief Engineer Sparrow, cursing the way his engines were being mistreated, responded as fast. Quickly the strain came off the shored-up collision bulkhead for'ard. Theakston shouted across the wheelhouse at Kemp.

'Just what I feared likely!' He had spoken to Kemp's retreating back: the Commodore was on his way down the ladder, making for the site of the damage. On the way he was joined by Cutler and Napper, the latter white around the gills and moving with obvious reluctance to put himself behind the bulkhead where the danger lay.

Kemp reached the fo'c'sle door and went down the ladder into the compartment abaft the collision bulkhead. There was total confusion: he found Amory and the hands standing in around three feet of water, with more welling up from the starboard lower corner of the bulkhead, where one of the shoring beams lay snapped in two and half submerged, broken right away from the metal that it should have been sustaining. There was blood on the water, and Kemp saw two men supporting another of the hands, holding the head above the level of the water. The man was dead: the head was stove in and brain matter was oozing through the hair.

Sickened, Kemp looked away. 'What happened?' He asked Amory. 'A gradual weakening, or – '

'I reckon it was more than that,' Amory said. 'I can't say for sure, but there could have been floating ice, broken pack ice. We're likely to get plenty of that from now on.'

147

Kemp nodded; from the bridge no floating ice had yet been seen, but with the snow still driving down so thickly it could have been obscured from sight as it drifted past. And a big wave could perhaps have smashed a sizeable block of it against the already weakened bulkhead. A quick visual examination had already shown up a number of sheared rivets. Kemp asked, 'Any hope of controlling it, Amory? How about the pumps?' He could hear the pumps in motion but was not surprised when Amory said they were being overtaken by the water pouring through. Even since Kemp had arrived on the scene, the level had deepened by a matter of three inches or so. He saw nothing that could be done for the moment: already, under Theakston's orders, the *Hardraw Falls* was swinging round across the sea, back once again to a sternwise progress. Once she was round and steadied, Amory said, he would wait till the pumps had overcome the reduced inflow and then he would try to encase the lifted section of the bulkhead in the seaman's last hope, a cement box – the construction of a wooden framework around the damage and pouring in of enough general dunnage mixed with sand and cement to seal it off.

Kemp waited until the ship was turned and all the weight was once again off the bulkhead. As the water level came down, he returned to the bridge and put Theakston in the picture.

'One man lost, I'm sorry to say, Captain.'

Theakston said nothing but his look was formidable. Kemp moved away from him: he didn't want a barney over the man's death, for which he felt responsible. Had he not gone against Theakston's advice . . . but that was in the past and he had only responded to what he had seen as his duty to reach Archangel as fast as possible. In war, men died. That was axiomatic. But it didn't lift the lead weight from the Commodore's mind.

ii

The death made its presence felt throughout the ship. The man who had died was not in fact a particularly popular member of the crew; he had become known as something of a scrimshanker. But his death, the crunch of that shoring beam, had changed all

148

that and he had become a symbol, a focal point of the mounting unease that had permeated the fo'c'sle hands. To die in action was one thing, to die because a stuffed-shirt commodore thought he knew better than the Old Man was quite another. It had been an unnecessary death and there might well be more, since there was still a party standing by the collision bulkhead and, according to the acting bosun, would remain there even after the cement box had been set up. Anything might happen at any moment, and most of the seamen would at one time or another find themselves taking a turn at bulkhead watch.

'And balls to that for a lark,' one of them said – the closed-face Londoner with a nasty twist to his mouth, Able Seaman Swile.

'Nothing we can do about it, mate. . . .'

'I dunno so much. We can make representations, can't we?'

'Fat lot of good!'

'Worth a go. Not to Amory or the Old Man. The bloody Navy, what was responsible in the first place.' Swile didn't say any more just then, he kept his own counsel until a propitious moment. He had his sights set on Petty Officer Napper, who had spent the voyage looking as disgruntled as a caught herring, the more so since his sad encounter with the metal rim of the wash-port. Napper had just the sort of fed-up look that said he might be a willing co-operator.

Swile's moment came when Napper was seen coming down a ladder and making for the naval ratings' messroom. Swile but-tonholed him outside the door.

'Can I have a word, mister?'

Mister again; Napper nodded and managed a smile. 'Yer. What can I do for you?'

'Matter of me mate. The one what got it at the collision bulk-head.'

'Oh, ah? Mate of yours, was he, eh.? Sorry about that, son.'

'So are we all. We don't want no more.' There was truculence in Swile's tone and Napper stiffened slightly, scenting trouble in a biggish way. 'That Commodore, he don't know what he's doing, went against the Old Man's advice . . . so we heard.'

'Who's we?' Napper asked cautiously, moving closer to the door of the messroom.

'Me and me mates.'

'You representing them, like?'

149

'Yes. Round Robin.'

'Round Robin, eh? Round Robin my arse! In the Andrew we call it mutiny – '

'We're not bloody Navy, mister.'

'Maybe not. I am. And you're under the Commodore's discipline and he's a rocky – RNR. A decent bloke too.' Napper might be chokker with this trip, but he resented criticism of Kemp and the Navy. 'Know something, do you? If two or more persons sign a request form – that's to say, if the request isn't made by one man as an individual – then we calls it mutiny. A mutinous gathering, see? Even though only on paper.'

Swile sneered. 'Load of crap is that.'

'Laid down in King's Regulations, crap or not.'

Swile lifted a bunched fist and waved it at Napper's nose. 'You just pass on what I said. It's not just you bloody Navy lot. It's that Nazi. All this is because he's aboard. You can't deny that. No one can. We don't want our lives put at risk for a fucking Nazi.'

'Well,' Napper said hastily. 'I see your point, of course, but don't you bloody involve me.' He dodged the threatening fist and managed to open the messroom door and slide to safety. Once inside he sank down on the bench running alongside the mess table and blinked in agitation. He found his hands were shaking. Mutiny was very, very nasty and although Napper didn't know quite how it worked out aboard a merchant ship he did know he had to shift the buck very quickly indeed, and that meant having another word with Cutler and being rather more forthcoming than last time. Cutler had seemed already to have a suspicion so he would have a ready ear.

After allowing the disaffected seaman time to bugger off, Napper climbed to the bridge. Arrived there, he sensed an atmosphere: ructions between Kemp and Theakston? Not his business. He approached Cutler and saluted through the driving snow.

'Mr Cutler, sir?'

'What is it, Petty Officer Napper?'

'What we was talking about earlier sir. What you asked me about – '

'Right! Go on, I'm listening.'

Napper reported the conversation with the crew member. Cutler asked, 'He approached you, did he?'

'Yessir.'

'What for?'

Napper stared. 'I just said, sir. Round Robin ... from the ship's crew like – '

'Yes. But what precisely was he asking?'

There was a longish pause, then Napper said, 'I – I dunno, sir.'

'He must have asked something.'

'Yessir. But – '

'He didn't say and you didn't ask. I'd have expected better than that of a PO. Wouldn't you?'

'Yessir. No, sir.' Napper, flustered now, felt his face going red beneath the layers of wool that almost obscured it. Bloody little ponce, young enough to be his son, talking to him like that. He'd been daft not to have approached the Commodore: the ship wasn't RN and Kemp, he wasn't the pusser sort who'd turn his back on a rating who addressed him direct rather than through proper service channels.

'Well?'

In a surly tone Napper said, 'He spoke of the prisoner, that's all I know, sir. Point is, the crew's upset about that bloke being lost for'ard. They don't think it should have happened.'

'What's that got to do with the prisoner?'

'I dunno, sir.'

'H'm.' Silence; the *Hardraw Falls* moved slowly backwards towards her Russian landfall, nearer and nearer to the nastiness, as Napper saw it, of Comrade Stalin's iron fist. You couldn't blame the crew for being uneasy. Napper was uneasy too, for all sorts of reasons – the Nazi himself, the damage to the ship and the resulting danger, the likelihood of further German attack, and his own personal problem which in the end might mean an enforced visit to a Russian quack after all. Cutler ended the silence abruptly. 'All right, PO. Ears to the ground and report as necessary. Do a little discreet probing, and in the meantime I'll have a word with the Commodore and Captain Theakston. What was the man's name?'

Oh, bugger, Napper thought. He said woodenly, 'I dunno, sir.'

'Jeez!'

Theakston said, 'It sounds like Swile. Able seaman. A bolshie sort.'

'Dangerous?' Kemp asked.

Theakston nodded. 'Aye, he could be. This sort of thing's always potentially dangerous – but I don't need to tell you.' He gave one of his rare smiles. 'You'll have to forgive me, Commodore. Your RN cap badge keeps on making me forget you're one of us basically. The grey-funnel lads look at things differently.'

'I know what you mean,' Kemp said. In the RN discipline was maintained, at any rate in the gate-and-gaiters world of the capital ships, under the overall threat of the Naval Discipline Act and King's Regulations; merchant shipmasters had no such sanction to back them up beyond a bad discharge at the end of the voyage. Discipline had to be maintained by the sheer force of personality of the master and his officers, maintained over a crew that was much more individualist than any warship's company.

Theakston broke into Kemp's thoughts. 'They see a Jonah. That's obvious.'

'Yes. Von Hagen – equally obviously.'

'I'd watch it if I were you, Commodore.'

'In what way?'

'Why, the Nazi. There could be trouble.'

'You don't mean they might try to get him?'

Theakston nodded. 'That's exactly what I mean.'

Kemp gave an incredulous laugh. 'That'd be madness, sheer insanity! They wouldn't have a hope in hell – '

'I don't know so much. A concerted attack, a rush of men against your sentry. Would you open fire, Commodore, if that happened? Somehow I don't think you would.'

Kemp said, 'We'll cross that bridge if we come to it. I don't believe we will, not for a moment. What would be the point, anyway?'

Theakston shrugged. 'Aroused passions don't always worry about a point, do they? I could quote many an instance ... if Swile stirs them up to it, I'd not call it impossible by a long chalk.

Of course, I agree with what you said just now – madness. It would be. We'd not get much of a reception in Archangel, not from the British, not from the Russians. But I never underestimate the destructive power of Jonahs, Commodore – ' He broke off. 'I'm teaching my grandmother again!'

'Grandmother,' Kemp repeated in a curious tone, and Theakston gave him an enquiring look. 'I happen to have a grandmother.'

'Still alive, d'you mean?'

'Yes. Old, of course, very old. Seafaring background – my grandfather and great-grandfather were both square-rigged masters.'

'Uh-huh?'

Kemp said, 'She believed in Jonahs, too. She'd heard so many stories. So have I – from her. Many times. She's got repetitive in her old age.' Kemp's thoughts, by a natural mental process, had gone back across the lonely, bitter sea to the cottage in Meopham. In the last conversation he'd had with Mary, on the phone back in Oban, she had hinted that his grandmother wasn't too good, feeling the cold ... He brought himself back to the present, sharply. 'Very well, Captain. I'll have my ratings alerted.'

iv

Swile had done a lot of talking around the ship, having worked himself up into an inflamed state of mind. His words had penetrated and all hands were thinking hard thoughts about the Nazi agent. Swile had hinted, no more so far, that the ship would be better off without him. He was received with jeers: sure, the ship would be better off without a Jerry aboard, but what could be done about it? Why worry anyway? There wasn't far to go now to Archangel, and the rumour said the Nazi was to be handed over to the Russians.

'Bloody likely I don't think,' Swile said, thumping a fist down on the mess table. His face was blue with the cold: he'd just come in from a turn at the collision bulkhead, surrounded by all that frozen metal and a slop of water from time to time that froze immediately it had entered and turned the compartment into a skating rink. There was a bruise on Swile's cheek where, as the result of a skid, he had impacted against one of the shoring beams. 'Buzzes . . . they're not always right, we all know that. Put around deliberate, half the time. Stands to reason, they're not going to hand a Nazi spy over to the Russians – he'll be wanted in UK.'

'So what? Where do we come in?'

'We don't want the sod aboard all the way home, that's what. For one thing – look, he's a kind of bloody magnet, right? The Jerries'll want him back. We know that – there was that Jerry cruiser. That won't be the only try, will it? Homeward bound, they'll be waiting for us, the whole bloody German fleet will!'

Swile spent the greater part of his off-watch hours that afternoon in persuasion, elaborating on the threat posed by the Nazi's presence aboard. Hook the German away, he said – surprise the Naval sentry, that wouldn't be difficult – then he remembered he'd spoken of the German to that Napper. Well, he could cover that, stop any extra guard by having another word with Napper and disperse any anxieties. He went on: hook von Hagen out of the cabin. But not just yet. They would wait till the ship was almost into Archangel and the attention of the Commodore and his assistant was on the business of safe entry through the ice, then they would attack.

And then what?

Hide the Nazi away, Swile said. Hide him and then at the right moment produce him, but produce him into Russian custody. With Russian port officials, and probably the secret police, aboard they couldn't go wrong. Kemp wouldn't have a chance. The Russians would be grateful and the *Hardraw Falls* would be free of its Jonah. And by the time they joined a homeward convoy, von Hagen's delivery would be bound to have become known to the Nazis and there would be no special attention paid to the ship. So what about it?

Nothing about it was the general verdict: Swile had gone round the bend. Where could you hide a bloke so he wouldn't be found? You wouldn't have a hope. It wasn't as though he could be nabbed and hustled away unnoticed. There would have to be a fight to get him out of naval custody.

'Just you wait,' Swile said.

The cement box had been constructed and Amory reported that the collision bulkhead could take more strain. They were able to move a little faster. But Theakston was adamant that his ship would not be turned back again. They must make the best way they could astern. By this time the *Hardraw Falls* was only about some eighty miles from the entry to the White Sea – say, thirteen hours' steaming at their new speed – with another two hundred and forty miles to Archangel itself through enclosed waters. There had been no further enemy attacks and Kemp believed they were safe now in that regard.

'Fingers crossed, though,' he said.

'Aye. The snow's thinning. We're going to be visible again if there's anything around.' Theakston lifted his binoculars and examined what there was of a horizon. There wasn't much but it was tending to extend as the snowfall lessened. He looked down at his decks: the ship was a moving snowdrift, with the stuff piled everywhere, thickly, half-way up the after end of the central island superstructure and against the fo'c'sle, with the windlass kept as clear as possible and in working order so that the anchors could be used if necessary as they made the final port approach. As well as the snow, there was ice in plenty, so much topweight of it that the ship was a little below her marks. The wind was still bitter, painfully so to exposed flesh. Inside his thick gloves, Theakston's fingers were numb, no feeling in them at all other than a dull pain like toothache. His feet were the same: Russian convoys, he thought, you can keep them . . . as so often on this trip he thought again about his wife. No news, nothing at all, the lot of any seaman in wartime, and it was no use hoping for any on arrival at Archangel either. The PQ convoy itself was carrying the mail and no more would come through until the next sailing from a UK port. They would all have to wait for that. The ship was likely to be in Archangel for the whole of the winter now: the collision bulkhead and the torn bows would have to be repaired and at any moment the ice would close the port and that would be that.

Theakston had spoken of this to Kemp. Kemp said it would be

a pound to a penny the *Hardraw Falls* would be left with a care and maintenance party while the rest of the crew and the naval contingent were entrained for Murmansk to take passage in the next homeward convoy.

'And von Hagen?' Theakston had asked.

Kemp said heavily, 'What happens to him depends on our naval liaison staff in Archangel. I don't seen any hope for him.'

'Anything more from Napper?'

'He seems to think it's died down.'

'Von Hagen'd be better off left to my crew! Better than the Russians.'

'Perhaps. But that's not a philosophy we can afford to indulge in, Captain.'

Theakston, recalling that conversation now, thought again about his sick wife: he couldn't afford to spend the winter iced up in Archangel with Dora on her own and missing him, but the ship had to have an officer left in charge. Maybe Amory ... Amory had no home ties. But, of course, that wouldn't be Theakston's decision. Once his owners had been informed of the situation, orders would come through and he just had to wait. Kemp would be all right: they wouldn't leave a convoy Commodore kicking his heels in a Russian port.

Throughout the ship, as the end of the outward run loomed, others were having similar thoughts of news and home. Cutler wondered if he might pick up those slender threads with Roz. There could be a chance; if there wasn't, well, there would be other girls looking for a good time in the midst of war, chasing that good time avidly, in fact, in case it was the last they ever had.

Petty Officer Napper was wondering how long the swelling was going to last: he didn't want to go home with *that*, though it would be nice to have the comforts and the wife's attention to his many ills. He was wondering, too, if he would be able to re-stock his cure-all kit in Archangel. Or even if it would be wise: the coms could have some weird ideas on medicine for all he knew, they were a primitive lot and probably unhygienic with it. But he was getting short of aperients, and that was important. The Russians must have something in that line, even if it was only old-fashioned stuff like Gregory powder, or liquorice powder, or Epsom salts or such ... Napper's wife swore by Epsom salts but

Napper himself found them not strong enough unless you took a triple dose and that was painful to say the least, talk about griping pains in the stomach! Once, Napper hadn't been for a fortnight, during which he had taken everything he could think of but with a nil result, and then at last he'd taken an enormous dose of Epsom salts that acted as a catalyst, making the last fourteen days' aperients explode together in one God Almighty go.

Napper was thinking about this when he stepped gingerly out on to the open deck. The ice was hell and very dangerous but could be negotiated so long as you kept a tight grip on the lifelines, and exercise was necessary to help keep things working internally. Moving along the starboard side of the after well-deck, past the cargo hatches invisible under the lying snow, he saw that the visibility had increased a good deal and the snow was coming down thinly and half-heartedly although still propelled against his body by that terrible east wind, a wind that had never agreed with him and always made him feel more out of sorts than was his norm.

Then, dimly through the overcast that was still with the ship, he saw the loom of a vessel away off the starboard bow. He gave a yell towards the bridge just as Cutler had reported to the Commodore. A moment later there was the flash of a signal lamp from the unknown ship.

On the bridge, Leading Signalman Corrigan reported the challenge. 'One of ours, sir!'

'Make the reply,' Kemp said.

Corrigan sent out the answer to the challenge and then reported, 'She's made her pendant number, sir. *Neath*, sir.'

One of the cruiser escorts. 'A little late,' Kemp said unsteadily, but there was enormous relief in his voice.

'She asks, do you require assistance, sir.'

For form's sake Kemp lifted and eye at Theakston, who gave a shrug. Kemp said, 'Make: "Thank you but do not require assistance currently. Glad to have you standing by should I need a tow."'

After Kemp's signal had been acknowledged, and the lean lines of the cruiser had become fully visible, more signalling came across. The convoy had been diverted into Murmansk and the battleships and cruisers of the Home Fleet had engaged the

German heavy ships; there had been losses on both sides but the German force had broken off the action and steamed away to the south, shadowed by a cruiser squadron. The remainder of the PQ escort had entered Murmansk with the main body of the convoy.

Kemp said, 'All's well that ends well, if you'll forgive the cliché.'

'It's not ended yet,' Theakston said.

'You mean von Hagen?'

'Aye! And him apart, there's nowt so daft as complacency.'

Kemp felt reprimanded, and was to have cause to remember Theakston's words.

SIXTEEN

Theakston brought down his glasses. He said, 'Cape Kanin, dead ahead. And dead on my ETA. I'll be altering course when we're off Kiya. Plenty of time yet.'

Kemp nodded, studying the seas ahead. The visibility was a lot better now; the snow had stopped altogether a few hours before, and for a while before that there had been nothing more than occasional flurries. The wind remained, as did the biting cold. There had been more drifting ice through which the stern of the *Hardraw Falls* had pushed at her painfully slow speed. All in all, Kemp thought the PQ had been the most worrying, the most frustrating convoy he had ever been with. The slow progress had been agonizing and the presence aboard of von Hagen seemed to have distorted everything away from the normal run of convoys. Not long after his conversation with Theakston, Petty Officer Napper had made another report, somewhat ostentatiously showing how dedicated he was to his duty.

'That there Swile, sir.'

'Yes?'

'Acting furtive, sir.'

'In what way?'

'Just furtive like, sir. Talking to the others out of the corner of his mouth . . . looking around first.'

'But without noticing you?'

'Yessir. Kept meself hidden, sir. Or anyway, looking as though I was doing something else and not aware of him.'

'Very cloak-and-dagger,' Kemp said, tongue in check.

'Beg pardon, sir?'

'Never mind, Napper. Carry on the good work, that's all.

Have you any definite ideas yet, any clue as to what Swile might be preparing to do?'

'No, sir, not yet, sir.'

'Very well.' Kemp made a dismissive gesture; Napper saluted and left the bridge. He would have liked to do some closer eavesdropping on Swile, but so far hadn't found a way of achieving this. Swile clammed up whenever he caught a sight of the naval ratings and short of disguising himself as a ventilation shaft there was no way Napper could get up close at the right moment. Being honest, Napper didn't see what Swile could possibly do; it was too late in the voyage, for one thing, they were coming right slap into enclosed Russian waters now, would soon have the communist land mass right around them, which was a terrifying thought in itself and never mind Swile and von Hagen. It was giving Napper the shivers: Stalin, the Man of Steel, was a real bully boy and by all accounts Russia was a joyless place at the best of times, all snow and ice and east wind and hunched-looking foodless peasants dressed in old sacks and such and fur hats – he'd seen shots on the newsreels in the Apollo cinema in Albert Road in Southsea, the posh part of Pompey, though Albert Road itself wasn't posh – but a sight posher than bloody Russia had looked like! Napper would heave a sigh of genuine relief when he was west of the North Cape again and heading south. The Russians could keep the *Hardraw Falls* so long as they parted with Petty Officer Napper . . . which in worrying fact they just might not. You never knew with dictators, they were so filled with a sense of their own importance that they thought they could get away with anything and, possession being nine parts of the law so to speak, Stalin might go and impound all hands once they were in his net with the hammer and sickle being brandished over them.

Bloody communists!

Napper had always voted Conservative: there was no mucking about with the Conservatives, they understood class differences and were a bolster to Napper's position as a petty officer, above the common herd of seaman. With the coms, all were equal, so Napper understood. Why, they even called their admirals Flagmen, just as though they were stokers or supply assistants! Napper recalled the programme for the fleet review back in 1937, for the coronation of King George VI . . . the USSR had sent along the old 23,000-ton battleship *Marat*, with a daft-looking bent-back fore funnel that was said to keep the fumes away from the bridge and foretop – anyway, she had carried an admiral, Flagman Ivanov.

For all Napper knew, Flagman Ivanov could be lurking in Archangel . . . maybe this Ivanov could even have come to the Pompey review as a spy and knew that Napper voted Conservative and never mind the sanctified secrecy of the ballot box.

Napper's jaws worked like those of an old-age pensioner without teeth. He was getting himself into a panic and that would never do – he was talking bollocks to himself, of course he was. Nevertheless, the awful feeling of doom persisted as the *Hardraw Falls* crept on arse backwards, as he put it, and came inshore of Cape Kanin, pushing into the White Sea and more ice that cracked and banged and scraped along her sides, making her sound like a drum gone wrong. By this time Napper had a full view of actual Russia for the first time in his life, only a fragment of it, of course, but quite enough.

Slowly, the ship slid on into the White Sea: twelve thousand tons of high explosive, a Nazi agent, a crew showing signs of a cack-handed mutiny, and the continuation of Napper's own personal problem that was defying his reduced stock of lanolin.

ii

'Ship approaching from ahead!'

The shout came down from the lookout in the crow's nest. Kemp called back, 'Can you identify?'

'Looks like an ice-breaker, sir.'

Theakston said, 'Clearing a channel. We're going to need it by the look of things.' By this time they were acting as their own ice-breaker, not very effectively since all they had to push with was the stern. To go through ice you needed not only a nice sharp bow but a heavily reinforced one at that, such as the proper ice-breaker would have. The *Neath*, however, had moved ahead of the *Hardraw Falls* and was doing her best to clear some sort of fairway. Both Theakston and Kemp knew they were only just going to beat the big freeze, the total ice-up of the port – beat it inwards, that was. If there had been a normal turnround they

161

would have beaten it outwards too, most likely, but the damaged bow had put paid to that prospect.

'Ice-breaker signalling, sir,' Corrigan reported some minutes later. 'From British Naval Liaison Officer Archangel to Commodore: "Intend to board. I shall approach your starboard side."'

'So BNLO's come out in person,' Kemp murmured. 'I wish us both luck!' To Corrigan he said 'Acknowledge.'

'Aye, aye, sir.'

Cutler, standing in the bridge wing with the Commodore, said, 'This is where it starts, sir. Von Hagen.'

'Yes. The interrogation, I imagine, while we go on for Archangel.'

'And the hand-over. . . .'

Kemp nodded, his face set into hard lines, deep clefts from the corners of his mouth. The dirt had come home to roost, or was about to. It went right against all his principles but, despite his promise to von Hagen, he saw no way out. Perhaps he had been wrong to make that promise, wrong to lift the man's hopes, but the promise had been only to try his best, nothing more, and he could still do that whatever the abysmal chances of success. In any case, von Hagen was an enemy with, apparently, a record of dirt on his own account. Kemp said. 'When they come alongside, Cutler, go down and meet BNLO. He's to be taken to my cabin and he's not to contact von Hagen in the meantime.'

'Very good, sir.' Cutler gave one of his American-style salutes and left the bridge. The Russian vessel was not so far off now; Theakston had passed orders for a ladder to be put over on the starboard side, from the fore well-deck, and Cutler went down to stand by with Amory and four seamen of the ship's crew, among them Able Seaman Swile. By now the *Hardraw Falls* had stopped engines so as to make it easier for BNLO to jump for the ladder and climb aboard, and was drifting slowly through the ice under what was left of her sternway.

There was a crunching sound as the ice-breaker moved closer, and great broken floes of ice surged up between the two hulls. From the bridge Kemp saw BNLO as he took him to be – an officer wearing the gold oak-leaved cap of a commander or captain. 'He's come with plenty of company,' he remarked to Theakston. There was an unidentifiable muffled figure and three seamen of the British Navy, armed with rifles and bayonets, plus another rating, obviously a signalman since he was carrying a battery-fed Aldis lamp and two hand flags for sending semaphore. Also waiting their turn to leap for the dangling rope ladder were two uniformed Russians who had the look of the OGPU, and a civilian in a vast fur hat, pulled down low over a dead white face with a slit for a mouth.

'I don't like the look of that bugger,' Kemp said as he looked down from the bridge. Unkindly, he had a hope that the man would miss the ladder and plunge into the cracking ice. But none of them did that; they came over the side behind BNLO and stood in a group in the well-deck as the ice-breaker moved away. Kemp saw Cutler salute BNLO and have a few words with him before turning for'ard and leading the way up the ladder to the central island and on up to the master's deck. The fur-coated Russian, Kemp noted, was having a good look around as he climbed and for an instant their eyes met. The Russian's, Kemp thought, were like those of a fish, cold and yet liquid.

A couple of minutes later Cutler came to the bridge.

'In your cabin, sir. Captain Brigger – BNLO, with a Lieutenant Phipps of the RNVR. And a Russian by the name of I. K. Tarasov.'

'H'm. What's his function, Cutler?'

'He's a colonel, sir. That's all BNLO said when he made the introductions. I guess he's probably secret police. He kind of looks that way.'

'So I noticed. All right, Cutler, I'll go down.'

Theakston asked, 'All clear to move on in, Commodore?'

'Yes, please. I'd be obliged if you'd let me know immediately if I'm wanted on the bridge, Captain. Never mind BNLO or I. K. Tarasov.'

'Right you are,' Theakston said.

Cutler asked, 'Do you want me with you, sir?'

'No, thank you, Cutler. If I do need you, I'll shout up the voice-pipe.' Feeling oddly and unusually nervous, Kemp clattered down the ladder to the master's deck and went into the alleyway. He glanced at the armed sentry on von Hagen's door and then went into his own cabin, outside which the British naval ratings and the uniformed Russians waited in a silent group, making way for the Commodore as he came up.

In Kemp's cabin, Captain Brigger and Colonel Tarasov were standing waiting with Lieutenant Phipps, now seen to have the

Special Branch green cloth between the gold rings of his rank. Kemp shook hands and said, 'I'd like to know to whom I'm speaking, Captain Brigger. Colonel Tarasov's function, I refer to.'

Brigger said, 'He's a special envoy, Commodore.'

'From?'

There was a nervous tic in BNLO's face, a twitch of a beetling eyebrow accompanied by a contraction of the puffy flesh below the right eye. He said, 'From the Kremlin. From Marshal Stalin, personally.'

Kemp nodded. 'Yes, I see.' He faced the Russian. 'Do you speak English, Colonel Tarasov?'

'I speak good English, yes.'

'That makes it easier, then.'

'You do not speak Russian.' It was more a statement than a question. Kemp said regretfully he had no Russian; Colonel Tarasov looked down his nose with something of a sneer: the English, his expression seemed to say, were uneducated.

'Please sit down, gentlemen. Er ... you'd like a drink, I expect?'

'Thank you, vodka,' Tarasov said.

'No vodka, I'm afraid. Gin?'

'Ah, gin. Very well, gin.' Tarasov made a face. BNLO and Phipps opted for gin-and-bitters. Kemp pressed his bell and Torrence entered the cabin with a clean cloth over his arm. He took the Commodore's order, which included whisky, and left the cabin with his usual brisk air, wishing he could linger outside the door after he'd served the drinks, but with such a mob around that wasn't possible, which was a pity. On the other hand, it was sometimes possible to overhear conversations in his pantry, which wasn't all that far from Kemp's cabin. There were interconnecting pipes and ducts that could carry sound, and even though there was interference from the hum of the forced-draught system Torrence's ears were sharp with much practice.

In the cabin BNLO started the ball rolling, glancing at his wristwatch as he did so. He had the look of a harassed man and one who had a good deal of work to do. 'You'll know why we're here, of course,' he said.

'Yes.' Kemp wasn't going to give him any help, was going to be non-committal, anyway at the start.

'You've had no trouble?'

BNLO obviously meant, trouble with von Hagen. Kemp said, 'No, no trouble.' He saw no reason to make anything of the abortive suicide attempt. The episode had been noted in the ship's log and his own log as Commodore of the convoy and in his view it had nothing to do with BNLO

'That's good,' BNLO said a little lamely. Kemp made a guess that Captain Brigger was as much out of his depth as he was himself: both of them were seamen, not diplomats or Intelligence agents. That would be the province of Lieutenant Phipps of the Navy's Special Branch – another guess and an obvious one now confirmed as correct by BNLO, who said, 'Phipps here – he has some questions to put. To von Hagen.'

Tarasov said, 'In my presence.'

'We've been into that,' Brigger said, twitching.

'I am adamant. I have taken note of what you said, Captain Brigger, and I am adamant.'

Brigger showed a line of yellowish teeth, briefly. He said, 'Like Stalin.'

'What was that?'

'Nothing – I'm sorry. Marshal Stalin is a strong man like you, Colonel Tarasov – '

'Yes.'

Kemp said, 'Would someone explain, please?'

'Yes – I'm sorry, Commodore. Colonel Tarasov wished – '

'Wishes.' Tarasov's narrow, peaked face was shoved forward.

'Wishes to be present when Phipps – er – talks to von Hagen. However, that's not in accord with my own orders from the Admiralty, as I have explained. But Colonel Tarasov is – er – '

'Adamant?' Kemp asked with the makings of a grin.

'Yes.'

'That's easily settled,' Kemp said. 'For now, von Hagen's in my charge. I'm responsible, and I shall not permit Colonel Tarasov to interview von Hagen at this juncture. I am adamant too.' He turned to Lieutenant Phipps. 'He's all yours. You may go to his cabin, alone.'

There was a tap at the door and Torrence came in with the tray of drinks and glasses.

'A little local difficulty I'd call it,' Torrence reported a few minutes later to Chief Steward Buckle, whose mind was once again
on caviar for the black market. Torrence had contrived to linger a
little outside the cabin door, appearing to tap on it but not allowing his knuckles to make contact until he'd heard some of the
natter. 'There's this Russki bloke, nasty little sod ... wants to
talk to the Jerry. Kemp, 'e won't have it. Got all hoity-toity about
it and raised 'is voice like. Now one of our blokes that come
aboard, RNVR officer, 'e's in the Jerry's cabin alone with him.'
Torrence paused. 'Course, that von Hagen's an old mate of
Kemp's, we know that.'

'Can't fall out with the Russians when you're in Russia, eh?'

Torrence scratched his head reflectively. 'Oh, I dunno. They
can't interfere with a British ship. International Law.'

'In time of war?'

'Dunno. I expect so, Chief.'

'You didn't hear any more?'

Torrence shook his head. 'No. Did me best, but no luck. Acou-
stics went off as you might say. Shame, that.'

Buckle went back to his calculations, trying to balance the
likely price of caviar in Archangel against what the market back
in UK would bear. Trouble was, the bloody Russians would
guess what he had in mind and would up the price to reduce his
profit margin.

Swile said, 'Came down from Buckle ... the buzz. Makes nasty
hearing.'

'What was it, then?'

'Kemp. He's gettting von Hagen in on the Old Pals' Act, see?
And I've bin doing a lot of thinking. Putting two and two
together. Those Russians that come aboard with the Navy ... I
reckon they've come for the Nazi and Kemp's not letting him go
in case he's in for a lousy time, which of course he is if the Russians get hold of him. And you know what that means: like I said
all along, the bugger comes with us, all the way to UK – right?'

Swile lit a fag and blew a trail of smoke. He was not blind to the obvious fact that the *Hardraw Falls* would be in Archangel for a full due; but, like Kemp, he believed that most of the crew would go home in another ship leaving ice-free Murmansk, and go home with von Hagen. So his anxieties remained.

'Don't see what anyone can do about it.'

'I'll be thinking,' Swile said. 'If the Nazi can be got out of that cabin, I reckon that's all we need do. The Russians'll do the rest. After all, we're in Russian waters, eh?' He left the fo'c'sle mess and went out to the fore well-deck. The *Hardraw Falls* was proceeding inwards through the channel cleared by the *Neath* and the ice-breaker, which had moved ahead of the British cruiser. Swile had gathered from one of the quartermasters that it was a long haul into Archangel itself, anyway at their current dead slow speed and moving astern. There should be time. Swile brooded: that Nazi had really got on his wick. He wanted to see him suffer and he knew the Russians would make him do that. Swile brooded on the past and what Mosley's thugs had done to him in London's East End in those prewar days, brooded on the years he'd spent in prison and the lessons he'd learned whilst inside, lessons not in going straight but in ways of getting even and causing damage to persons in the process. He'd had some tough companions in HM prisons, some tough enemies too, but he'd survived by the strength that had been in his own body and still was.

He looked towards the Russian coastline. The place was iron hard, grey dismal, oppressive – just the place for a Nazi to ponder on past misdeeds in the short time that would be left to him. Swile looked up at the bridge, saw Theakston looking aft from the wing, using his binoculars. That Cutler was with him. No sign of Kemp – he'd still be below, putting in his oar on the Nazi's behalf. Swile flung his arms about his body: he'd never known such cold. The crunch of the ice as the ship pushed her stern against it had a sound of doom and foreboding and ahead of the two British ships the Russian ice-breaker appeared to have slowed a little as if waiting for the *Hardraw Falls* to catch up.

SEVENTEEN

Lieutenant Phipps was a patient man; he'd learned patience in the corridors of the Foreign Office, the long career corridors that led to power. A prewar diplomat, Phipps had been specially commissioned into the RNVR without having to go through the often lengthy process of being commissioned from the lower deck. Phipps was a valuable man and since entering the Navy had added to his attainments a formidable ability to interrogate. He was a linguist and spoke both German and Russian amongst other languages. And he had an ability to make people trust him. He had a youthful face that belied his maturity and he looked honest: he had a happy smile, which currently he was using on von Hagen.

'Just a few words,' he said. 'You must see there's no reason why you shouldn't talk to me in the absence of Colonel Tarasov.'

'Before I'm handed over to him.'

'Well – yes. I admit that's the idea. Under certain circumstances, that is.' Phipps paused and held out his cigarette case. Von Hagen took one and Phipps leaned forward, flicking a light. 'I think you understand me, don't you, Colonel von Hagen?'

Von Hagen nodded. 'Oh yes. If I talk, I'll not be handed over. Commodore Kemp has already told me that.'

'Yes, of course. You and he – you knew each other before the war.'

'Yes, indeed we did.' There was an inward look in the German's eyes. 'They were good times. . . .'

'But you haven't told Commodore Kemp anything, have you?'

'No.'

Phipps smiled. 'He's not a good interrogator, is he? Not his line. But it's mine.'

'You mean – '

'I mean only that I'm in a position to help. I'm not suggesting ... anything crude. That can be left to the Russians, if you get that far. All I'm suggesting is that you take advantage of a kind of salvation. Not too strong a word, Colonel von Hagen. In Britain you'll be treated properly, and after the war you'll go back to Germany. If the Russians have custody of you – '

'Yes, yes, I know very well, you have no need to elaborate, Lieutenant Phipps.'

'Quite. Then perhaps you'll – '

'No.' The German shook his head.

'But surely – '

'No. If you ask the reason, it's this: I don't believe your promises. I believe that even if I talked to you, I would still be handed over to the Russians. I believe this because I know my own value to them, and also, and over-ridingly, because it is the Russians whose waters we are in and who have the whip hand.'

'Oh no. I assure you – '

Von Hagen made a dismissive gesture. 'Your assurances ... no! You will tell me that pressures would be put on the Kremlin by Whitehall, that Winston Churchill himself would erupt like a volcano over his cigar, that the course of the war would be inter-rupted in the interest of my salvation. All that would be words only. Matters would not happen that way. I am not a fool, Lieu-tenant Phipps.'

'I never suggested you were, though I had hoped ... how-ever, there's something else.' Phipps looked away for a moment. 'You never married, Colonel.'

'No.'

'But there was someone in London, before the war called you away.'

Von Hagen's face went white and he jerked a little, but he said nothing.

'Marie-Anne de Tourville. A Frenchwoman.' Phipps stubbed out his cigarette half smoked. He lit another and blew smoke towards von Hagen. 'She's still there. Completely unmolested, but under surveillance.'

'Why under surveillance? She was never a Nazi sympathizer, that was separate from my activities, she knew nothing – '

'We know that, Colonel. She's clean.'

'Then – '

Phipps smiled. 'She can be brought in on suspicion. We can do that at any time. We can always find charges.'

'Trumped-up, of course.'

'Of course. If you think that's dirty, have a good look at your own hands and Herr Hitler's, Colonel. Even the British can be beastly, you know, if pushed. We – '

'This, then, is the threat?'

Phipps said, 'Yes, I'm afraid so. I honestly don't like it, but there it is, I'm under orders from a certain department of state – '

'The monster Churchill?'

'Not the monster Churchill, and I'm surprised at you of all people falling for propaganda. Mr Churchill knows nothing of this – there are many things he has to be kept in ignorance of.' Phipps looked at his wrist-watch as if assessing how much longer he had before I.K.Tarasov began creating. 'If you don't answer the questions I shall put, then a message will go to London once we have reached Archangel. Mamselle de Tourville will be arrested on certain charges. She will be imprisoned without trial, held under Regulation 18b. She won't be comfortable, Colonel.' Phipps brought out a handkerchief and blew his nose. 'Matters could become, well, fairly extreme.'

ii

Kemp sat on in his cabin with Captain Brigger and I.K.Tarasov, the latter obviously furious at having been baulked – quite why, Kemp didn't really know: Tarasov's time was presumably to come unless he, Kemp, could find a way of keeping von Hagen aboard. The prospect of that looked so dim as to be invisible although Brigger could be an ally. But he would have no more effect than Kemp, probably – and of course he was under orders from the Admiralty even though he wouldn't be liking them any more than Kemp. Kemp and Brigger meanwhile chatted of this and that, of prewar days largely, innocuous stuff, reminiscences of ships that had gone already in the war, men whom both had known, naval officers with whom Kemp had served when doing his RNR time annually aboard a ship of the fleet. I.K.Tarasov listened, no doubt hoping to pick up an indiscretion. His face, Kemp thought, was like that of a rat: the fur collar and the fur hat, still on his head, gave him the appearance in fact of a rat peering out of a ball of oakum. . . .

The *Hardraw Falls* moved on.

Tarasov spoke. 'Your Lieutenant Phipps, Captain. He is taking a long time.'

'Yes, isn't he?' BNLO said in a pleasant tone. Tarasov's thin mouth clamped shut like a trap. He got to his feet, brushed impatiently past Kemp, and glared out from the square port at the barren sea and the desolate land sliding past in the distance. Maybe, Kemp thought, he was wondering if that terrible land was going to be so welcoming when he had to report that the British had interrogated von Hagen without his own presence, that he had been unable to shift the British Commodore. . . . All at once Kemp was seized with a hatred of the land he was approaching, a deep loathing of its totalitarianism, as bad as that of Adolf Hitler with his tantrums in Berchtesgaden or wherever. If I.K.Tarasov was typical of Stalin's secret police, which no doubt he was, then it would be a sordid act to hand over von Hagen, to deliver him into the hands of barbarism.

There was a tap at the door.

'Come in,' Kemp said. Tarasov turned round. One of the armed British naval ratings stood in the doorway. He addressed Brigger.

'Lieutenant Phipps, sir. He'd like a word. Just with you, sir.'

Brigger got to his feet, lifting an eyebrow at Kemp. 'All right, Commodore?'

Kemp nodded. 'Of course.' BNLO left the cabin. Tarasov went back to his study of land and sea.

iii

'Any luck, Phipps?'

'Yes, sir. In the end.'

'You used the woman angle, did you?'

'I did. I went the whole hog. As far as the death penalty.'

'On a charge of which she's wholly innocent.'

'Yes – '

'You're a hard customer, Phipps.'

'We have to be, sir. We're all bastards now, thanks to Hitler.'

'What did he tell you, Phipps?'

Phipps said, 'There are German agents operating inside Russia – that's not news to us, of course, and in a general sense it won't be news to Tarasov either. The point is, these are specially infiltrated agents and von Hagen has the names and where-abouts – and the orders. The orders are simple, very straightfor-ward. The agents are inside Russia to carry out an assassination.' Phipps paused for effect. 'Guess who?'

BNLO's mouth tightened. 'Not – ?'

'Yes. Stalin. Stalin himself.'

'So that's why he has to be handed over!'

'It's vital to them,' Phipps said. 'If Stalin's knocked off, that gives Hitler his chance against a Russia *in extremis* – the Kremlin couldn't hope to hide it, not with all the hierarchy jockeying for position, in-fighting for the succession.'

'But why should the British government – how could the Kremlin have known – '

Phipps interrupted. 'My guess would be that the Kremlin has picked up a little but not enough. They don't know who, how or when. Von Hagen does. The Kremlin presumably knows he knows, hence the pressure on our war cabinet to cough him up.'

'Yes, I see.' The two officers were out on the open deck, in the bitter cold that currently they scarcely felt. BNLO walked up and down, with quick, rather nervous steps, with Phipps keeping step beside him. 'Has von Hagen given you the details, the full facts – names and so on?'

'Yes, he has.'

Brigger said, 'I don't see why he caved in on your threat about the woman – or rather, I don't see why he should believe you when you said she'd be left alone if he talked.'

'That's easy, sir. He knows she's not involved in anything, just as we do. We really haven't use at all for her other than as a lever. There'd be absolutely no point in *not* letting her go once he'd talked – he knows that.' Phipps added, 'We were just going to be – er – '

'Complete and utter shits,' BNLO said, 'if he *hadn't* talked!'

172

'Yes, I'm afraid so. But now we haven't got to be. Not in regard to the woman.'

'And von Hagen? Surely we can pass his information to Tarasov ourselves?'

Phipps shook his head. 'There's no change in his position, sir. The orders were very precise: he's to be handed over in Archangel, whether or not he's talked to us. I know it's nasty, but it's war. The Russians want do some pumping of their own.'

'But – ' Brigger broke off suddenly as one of the ship's crew came up the ladder from the after well-deck, moving at the double, eyes staring in what appeared to be terror. He flung past Brigger shouting out something about a bomb, and went on past the master's alleyway to the bridge ladder, still shouting. The shouts penetrated Kemp's cabin, where Tarasov came away from the port like lightning, pushed his way out of the cabin, and yelled an order in Russian at the uniformed security police waiting outside. As Kemp came out from the cabin behind him, making for the bridge, he saw Tarasov and his armed bully boys approaching the sentry on von Hagen's cabin. Kemp, when he reached the bridge, saw that the man who had shouted was Swile and that caused him to smell a biggish rat. Seeing the Commodore's approach, Theakston called to him.

'Report of ticking alongside Number One hold, Commodore. If the report's right we may not have long to abandon – '

'Unless we find the object,' Kemp said. There was something in his tone that made Theakston look at him sharply and with a look of puzzlement. 'I'd be obliged if you'd leave this to me,' Kemp went on. Before quitting his cabin he had brought his revolver from the safe. Now he showed it, ostentatiously. 'All right, Swile. We're going on a bomb hunt, you and I.'

iv

It was no more than a hunch and Kemp was very aware of the risks as he went below to the tween-deck and the hatch leading to Number One hold with its cargo of high explosive. They could all vanish in one split second of fire and fury, all of them, Theakston and the bridge staff, the engine-room complement, BNLO, the Russians, von Hagen ... but Kemp felt pretty sure inside

173

himself. Bombs didn't appear all that suddenly after so long at sea from the Firth of Lorne, although it could perhaps be possible for a device to be so timed that it didn't start its tick until it was ready to detonate – but had there been no delays it would presumably not have gone off until some while after the Archangel arrival when it could have activated itself in a ship emptied of its cargo, not such a useful thing to do.

'Now,' Kemp said. 'Where is it, Swile?'

Swile put on a puzzled look. 'Dunno, sir. Seems to have stopped.'

'Yes, it does, doesn't it? You're an exceptionally brave man, Swile.'

Swile made an indistinct sound and looked warily back at Kemp. Kemp said pleasantly, 'You don't look at all scared, Swile. Not like a man who's about to be blown sky high.'

'That's cos it's stopped bloody ticking, innit?'

'Pull the other one, Swile. I didn't come down with the last shower! This has something to do with the German agent – right? I've had reports – '

'That bastard!' Swile said – almost screamed. His face was contorted with hate. 'Well, it worked, didn't it? I looked into the alleyway as we come past – the Jerry had been hooked out by the Russians – '

'Yes.' Kemp, too, had noted the fact. It had worked only too well, but even if it hadn't Kemp saw no way of keeping von Hagen aboard now. Dirt would have its course. 'All right, Swile. This will be gone into later. For now, get out of my sight – fast!'

Swile scuttled away. Kemp's face was savage as he climbed to the well-deck and went on up to the bridge. On the way he went into the master's alleyway and found Petty Officer Napper in red-faced argument with I.K.Tarasov.

'You'd no right,' Napper was saying. 'I'm in charge o' the prisoner – '

'Shut up.'

Napper bristled. 'Don't you speak to me like that, bloody civvy – '

'*Russian* civvy. You are in Russian waters.'

'Makes no difference! This is a British ship and you'd no right. Why, I – '

I. K. Tarasov went up close to Napper and stared at him with his fish-cold eyes. 'I am Colonel Tarasov. I am of the OGPU. I am powerful, and you are rude. If I lift my little finger – '

'Sorry, sir, I didn't know you was an officer, sir, I thought you was a civvy.'

'Yes. So now you will do as you are told by me, and shut up. Yes ?'

'Yessir!' Napper said, and saluted. Kemp went on towards the bridge. Napper had been so agitated that he hadn't seen the Commodore, and Kemp saw no point in interfering – there was nothing to interfere about, the whole thing was a *fait accompli* now, and he felt weary to death with the voyage and the intrigue. He had almost to drag himself up the ladder to the bridge. There had been so little sleep, so much anxiety, so many things continually on his mind. He found Cutler on the bridge, standing beside Theakston. Theakston was looking grimmer than Kemp had yet seen him, his face stiff as he glanced round at the Commodore's approach.

He said, 'It's all over.'

'Almost, yes.'

'I don't mean the voyage, Commodore. Brigger brought a signal from the Ministry of War Transport. It's only just been sent up.' Theakston's voice faltered for a moment and suddenly Kemp understood.

'Your wife, Captain?'

'Dead,' Theakston said. 'Three days ago ... while we were flogging along the Kola Inlet. So many bloody miles away ... not that it would have made any difference.'

Kemp found no words to say. He laid a hand on Theakston's shoulder and squeezed. His heart seemed like a ball of lead. Theakston's voyage had been no easier than his own, and now landfall had brought its bombshell. It had always been Kemp's own fear that something would happen to Mary while he was away at sea. Theakston turned away and went into the wheel-house. Kemp remained where he was, with Cutler.

'That's rotten,' Cutler said.

'Yes.' Kemp pushed it to the back of his mind : it had to be just one of those things and the *Hardraw Falls* was not far off the final stretch into Archangel. 'What's up with that ice-breaker, Cutler ?'

Cutler brought up his binoculars. 'Stopped, sir.' A moment later the Russian began signalling and Corrigan read it off.

'Well?' Kemp asked.

'Stuck, sir. Stuck in the ice.'

Theakston had heard. He passed the order to stop engines. Already, ahead of them, the cruiser escort was turning under full helm, beating it out before she stuck fast for the winter, her signal lamp busy as she moved past.

Corrigan reported, '*Neath* to Commodore, sir: "I will wait outside the ice boundary."'

'Acknowledge. Add: "Much obliged but don't bother."'

'Aye, aye, sir.'

Cutler said, 'I guess he expects us to move out, sir – not to enter, but –'

'Yes. But I think he's over hopeful, Cutler. The damage – and the question of fuel. There may be a tanker in Murmansk, I suppose.'

'If we could do it –'

'If we could do it, Cutler, we could keep von Hagen and have the additional bonus of I.K. Tarasov. But that's being over hopeful too. In any case, there'd be a Russian warship waiting for us off the Kola Inlet.' Then Kemp added, 'But I don't think we're going to make it out anyway. Look down there.' He gestured down the ship's side, and then astern. There were great chunks of broken ice tumbling in the wake of the departing cruiser and even as Kemp and Cutler watched the chunks froze into a solid, rocky mess, while similar things happened along the sides of the *Hardraw Falls*. A moment later the ship crunched to a full stop.

v

'Just our bloody luck!' Napper said some motionless hours later. 'God knows when we'll get back to UK now.' He glowered down at the solid freeze, which linked them all with Archangel still many miles ahead. 'I wonder if the buggers'll send a quack out if Kemp asks for one?' He was speaking to Able Seaman Grove, past impertinences forgotten in his hour of anguish. He was standing with his legs apart: it eased the ache a little, pressure was not a good thing, and when he moved it was still crab fashion.

Grove said, 'Dunno, PO. If they do they'll likely take you to hospital, I shouldn't wonder.'

'No! In bloody *Russia*?'

'Grove grinned. 'Where else?'

'They're not getting me off of this ship! This ship's England as far as I'm concerned.' Petty Officer Napper gave a sound like a bleat and went below where he could no longer see Russia. If you tried, if you didn't look, you might fool yourself in the end and of course with any luck they mightn't have long to hang about, but his knackers could hardly wait till they made contact with civilization again. Before BNLO had gone ashore, or anyway gone down to the ice to embark aboard what looked like a horse-drawn sleigh, he'd assembled the crew and the naval party and told them he would make arrangements, or hoped he could, for such hands as could be spared to be transferred across the ice to Archangel and the train for Murmansk and a homeward convoy, but it might take time since they would have a low priority. . . . Napper prayed that BNLO's efforts would be successful. In Napper's view the shore party had looked a right lot of Charlies setting off behind a horse, and the OGPU man had looked furious, in just the mood to tear strips off the local weathermen who'd been caught out by the advance of the ice. With Tarasov had gone the German spy and bad luck to him. Napper had been on deck when the party had left and he fancied he would never forget the look in Kemp's face as von Hagen went over the side. Odd, that; such a hoo-ha over a rotten Nazi, just as though he'd been the Commodore's brother or something. . . .

Napper rooted about in his medical stores and went off into a loud moan. One more squeeze and that would be the end of the lanolin.